The Crazy Psychologist

by

Miller Caldwell

Matador
9 Priory Business Park,
Wistow Road, Kibworth Beauchamp,
Leicestershire. LE8 0RX
Tel: (+44) 116 279 2299
Fax: (+44) 116 279 2277
Email: books@troubador.co.uk
Web: www.troubador.co.uk/matador

ISBN 978 1910667 248

British Library Cataloguing in Publication Data.
A catalogue record for this book is available from the British Library.

Printed and bound by CPI Group (UK) Ltd, Croydon, CR0 4YY

Matador is an imprint of Troubador Publishing Ltd

For Laura

Dr Laura Elizabeth Caldwell B.Sc (Hons Glasgow) D.Clin. Psy. (Staffordshire & Keele Universities). Now working at the residential unit of the Moseley Children's Hospital, Birmingham.

In Memoriam

F.Scott Dunbar
1972-2014
A trusted friend to so many.

Contents

Martial the things for to attain
The happy life be these I find:
The riches left, not got with pain:
The fruitful ground, the quiet mind.

The Happy Life
Henry Howard, Earl of Surrey 1517-1547.

Author's Disclaimer

Those who read my books no longer ask whether the characters and places are real. They prefer to ask whether such bizarre events in my life actually happen.

The setting of this novel is on Orkney where I have distant relatives and I have visited the historic island not so long ago. I trust I may be welcomed back to the Orkney Isles by those who have read this book.

The rest are composites of real places, events and people and just now and then figments of my imagination which I think are real. This disclaimer has two purposes. Firstly it keeps me one step ahead of a punch on the nose from real psychologists. Secondly royalties earned on the sale of this book will pay for the sessions I have booked with my Clinical Psychologist. She tells me to expect several months of treatment due to a perceived worrying diagnoses.

For updates on writing, health and life's foibles, see the News section on www.netherholmpublications.com

Criticism, abuse, cheek or the occasional appreciation is welcomed. Send your comments to me at: netherholm6@yahoo.com

ACKNOWLEDGEMENTS

This is a novel dedicated to Laura but it is not based on her cases or notes or even her professional work in CBT (Cognitive Behavioural Therapy). However Laura is a clinical psychologist and she did inspire this novel. So the book is dedicated to her. The story stems from each page I write. This cannot be a book of any academic worth other than the chuckling and thought provoking moments it provides and all psychologists value a good belly laugh as therapy.

The Cornerstones Agency and the Society of Authors in Scotland provide unstinting support to me in all my novels. Special thanks go to Mollie Baxter whose eagle eye watched over Rousay and how the novel progressed with many helpful pieces of advice. Thanks especially to Richard Chalkley of Spiffing Covers who has provided the book cover and typeset the text. And to Matador Publishers who have brought this book to life.

Alan, Margaret, Stuart, Joyce, Danny, Katy, Morag, Ian, Mark, Don, Sean, Rachel and Jocelyn all have played a part in keeping my mind and body healthy. Jocelyn provides for all my other needs of which there are too many to mention. I could not survive without her.

Finally I remember with fond kindness and true friendship Scott Dunbar who knew this was my next novel. It saddens me that it will never be in his hands.

ONE

It was the last time Anthony Arnold would hear the heavy metal doors squeak and clang shut. They needed oil he had often thought, but prisons lacked lubrication. He had lived without many comforts for the past two decades and more. He got used to that. The parole board had seen positive changes in him however and he was about to be released. The day came. It was not a confident step after step he took as he progressed along the corridor, checking if it was safe to leave. When that tall old frameless wooden door welcomed him to the outside world it did so briefly, before being securely closed to retain his cellmates a wee bit longer.

He knew there would be no one on the outside to greet him on his departure. No relatives had visited for the past twenty six years. Few, if any, would have remembered the young father who murdered his wife. Balding and slightly overweight Tony stood outside Barlinnie Prison, Glasgow, closed his eyes and took a deep breath. It was the same breath he inhaled every morning about this time of day in the exercise yard but today when his eyes opened there were no walls. He turned back to look at his place of incarceration. He shook his head. Society had forgiven him but for what purpose now?

'Hey Tony, so how does it feel?' asked the driver of a green Mazda CX 5 which pulled up beside him. 'C'mon.

Get in.'

Tony opened the car door of his aftercare social worker Brian Levack and sat down. He looked transfixed at the coloured controls on his car's fascia. Brian saw his puzzled look. He lit up three yellow lights putting Tony's car seat at maximum heat.

'I've got a flat fixed for you. You'll like it. It's where we're heading. It's in an up and coming residential area, the Gorbals.'

Tony sat on his hands. 'My seat's burning I think.'

'Winter warming you mean. Most cars have them these days,' laughed Brian.

He withdrew his hands. The warmth was satisfying. But he was not at ease.

'The Glasgow Gorbals. God no. Not the Gorbals. That's a God forsaken part of town,' said Tony.

Brian knew where Tony was coming from. Indeed the Gorbals had had a reputation and Tony's needle was stuck in that groove.

'Not now. Modern one bedroom flats. There are a few old cons in some but it's up to you, who you meet.'

'Well, at least it's not Kilmarnock.'

'Why's that?' asked Brian.

Tony clasped his hands tightly. The blood disappeared leaving cold white knuckles.

'The scene of my crime.'

Brian recalled the details of his case notes. He nodded as if to agree.

'But you have no connection there now. We've been through that,' said Brian.

Tony stroked his clean shaven chin. 'You think I don't have family?' he said lowering his voice.

'That's what you told me, didn't you?'

'Aye, I did. But it's probably not true. I had a daughter and ....maybe a son....'

A lack of clear thinking may have been explained by his sudden release. Brian's role was to enable him to cope in his new surroundings. To do that he really had to know how his mind was working. He needed his co-operation.

'I see. So, any idea where they are? Could you contact them? In fact, I should make the introductions,' suggested Brian.

'They possibly stayed in Ayrshire. I don't know. If the girl married, I'll never find her anyway. The other kid? Maybe....maybe he didn't exist. Perhaps I made him up.'

Brian's furrowed brow eased as he opened his glove box and took out his Caro Emerald CD.

'Here, take out the disc and play it,' said Brian.

Tony ran his finger along the CD dashboard slit.

'You mean in here?'

♦

A young fresh-faced lass, masked behind a bunch of cut flowers, rapped on the front door. The oak door creaked open with hinges pained by the fresh sea-salt air.

'For Dr Angie Lawrence,' she announced.

'Again. Well, I suppose so,' he said taking hold of the stems and turning the flowers upside down as he offered his thanks. He noticed the flowers came from Interflora, in Perth this time.

Sam Lawrence closed the door of the stone cottage at Wasbister and walked through to the kitchen collecting scissors from the Welsh dresser as he proceeded to the 18th century outhouse. He cut the cellophane and held the card up for closer inspection.

'To Angie, with love xxx.'

Sam's eyebrows gathered. Clients and their parents showed their appreciation with baking, fruit sometimes but most regular of all, came the flowers. They came from flower shops all over the land, from the children's home towns as if troubled families had a network outdoing each other with belated kindness.

The trouble was that most of the vases in the house were already full of blooms. The dining room cupboard heaved with boxes of soft centres, chocolate Brazil nuts and Quality Street which sometimes accompanied the blooms. But never a tie or a set of six golf balls appeared. The gifts were always for his wife. Artists rarely receive any perks for their trade.

His wife, Dr Angie Lawrence, also in her mid-thirties, was a clinical psychologist. Her hair swept back in a luscious cushion of ash blonde. Her fingernails were coated in aquamarine blue and more often than not her zebra striped fashion spectacles sat at the end of her nose, balanced precariously to accentuate her blue eyes.

The couple had arrived six months earlier for Angie to run the new purpose-built twelve bed Hazelnut assessment centre on the Orkney Island of Rousay. Children were referred from all Scottish Authorities when anorexia, bulimia and social anxiety cases required further assessment and treatment.

The island had a population of just over 200 with almost an archaeological site for each inhabitant. The remoteness had bucked the trend of desertion. Families from south of the border were the new invaders masquerading as pioneers to their far-away relatives. It was a quiet island wakened each day by the wayward wind's howl and waves gushing where bubble bursting wireweed and floating canopies of kelp kept constant motion neither coming nor going.

Sam loved the laughing of the sea, the cries of the Great Skua and the whining of the grey seals. They posed an artistic challenge after years in industrial Lancashire where the humming of noisy traffic and the chatter of the streets had drained him of his industrial artistic talent. There too he had married Angie six years previously.

His new life on the quiet island gave him considerable peace of mind and creativity of brush. There was only one outstanding matter of concern to this bearded six foot three inch man, as thin as a broad stroke of his favourite paintbrush. His wife Angie was as enigmatic as ever and her antics were not always understood and rarely met with his complete satisfaction or agreement.

♦

'Meal ready?' asked Angie slamming the heavy front door behind her on her return from work.

'Almost,' replied Sam shouting from the kitchen where he had been shredding broad beans.

Angie went up to change. Off came one sweater for another. Off came one pair of slacks for another but she kept on her green and brown Ecco Mules. They lived on her feet. She returned to the kitchen skipping along the corridor like a teenage schoolgirl. She smiled as she passed the latest bouquet of vased flowers.

'So how's your day been?' she asked.

'Not much happened. Went for a walk to find a good view. Drew a few outlines, that's all. And you?'

'Fine,' said Angie, popping a small cherry tomato in her mouth.

'Oops, nearly forgot. No client talk,' recalled Sam.

'Hmm,' Angie swallowed the skin full of seeds. 'Anyway, got a young lad from Edinburgh today, Simon. He's an elective mute.'

'Suppose he's...a bit like me.'

'What do you mean?' asked Angie, turning to meet

her husband's eyes.

'All day long I contemplate. Keep my thoughts to myself. I can be silent for hours on end, you know.'

'Hours? That's not the same. This lad has not spoken for over two years,' she said throwing her hands in the air as if the two scenarios had anything in common.

'Perhaps he's got nothing to say,' Sam smiled as if he had made a revealing diagnosis. 'Oh, ...I almost forgot, more flowers.'

'Really? I really must be appreciated. Clients are making this work so enjoyable. That them on the window ledge?'

'Yup, that's them. I'm not surprised it's the last vase. You know it's hard to imagine such gratitude, I mean....'

'Goodness knows what will come next. I am popular aren't I Sam?'

Sam ignored her question. He turned to look at his wife. She held the mauve vase, sniffing the fragrance. Was this the loving, contented girl he met at a still life class in Manchester? Or was her maturity and now her responsibilities making her drift apart from him? Sam did not wish to lose her but he could not hold back his irritation with her outlook on life.

'Don't you think it's over the top, flowers, boxes of chocolate......?' he said.

'Jealous. That's what you are darling. You keep to your painting. And er...there seem to be a few Brazil nut chocolates missing. Did you enjoy them?'

Later that night as the dark clouds obliterated the last streaks of dark blue sky, they sat in the low ceilinged lounge with curtains open, framing the black ink of the sea. The back door jittered in the wind. They listened to Classic FM and Satie's Gymnopédie No 1.

Angie placed her hand on Sam's thigh.

'Romantic, isn't it?'

'What, Orkney or Satie?' clarified Sam.

'Both really. Half a year already and I feel at home here. And you?'

'We moved at the right time. It's certainly been good for my art.'

'And you love me still?'

'Yes..... still I love you, you crazy girl.'

Angie curled up on the settee like a sleepy child. Sam placed his arm round her in support. Then he ran his fingers through her long hair massaging her skull. She did not move, but smiled.

'Next week I have a doctorate programme student coming from Glasgow,' she informed him.

'You mean to supervise?'

'Yup, won't that be good?'

'For who?' asked Sam.

'For us both of course,' said Angie arching her eyebrows playfully at her husband.

TWO

The following day was a rare summer morning. The sky was a clear bright Murano glass blue and the sea managed only a gentle wave, making seaweed shiver on the breaking ripples. A warmth rose from the ground like an open fire and arctic terns darted here and there on random sojourns to announce a very fine day on Rousay indeed.

Sam left the cottage after his mid morning coffee and walked with his artistic paraphernalia along the main road for more than a mile till he was at the far eastern end of Saviskaill Bay. He turned right off the road and began the ascent to the high vantage point at Keirfea, over 229 metres. As he climbed, he passed some scattered and protruding white stones, the relics of prehistoric teeth he imagined.

Sweat trickled down his face as the sun and the climbing effort combined to dampen his handkerchief. He stopped for a brief rest. He turned back. Before him was the bay and beyond, the Westray Firth welcoming pleasure craft to explore the myriad of small islands in its web.

Silence, that city fearing feeling was playing games on Sam's mind as he set up his pad. He heard a small twig snap as he lowered himself into a comfortable position. He looked around. Not a tree was in sight. He held the twig up and studied it. He decided it must have been a bird's nest building twig which fell from its flight. Then once more that soft silence descended, keeping him safe from any loneliness.

His pencil drew a rough outline of the sweeping bay like a mighty bite from a prehistoric sea monster's teeth. The jagged grasses beyond the sand, danced a Schottische. Tricky to capture. And as ever, the rocks stood boldly as curtains of delicate waves nibbled at their edges.

He ate a sandwich of ham and mustard in a glycemic index roll at mid-day and after swigging from his lukewarm water bottle, he munched into a Tunnock's teacake. After a Cox's apple, Sam lowered his sunhat over his face to rest it lightly on his nose. He lay back and took twenty post-prandial winks.

Perhaps it was only eighteen winks but a certain human cry played on his mind. It was a contented excitement that he thought he heard. One which could be faintly detected by strained ears. The noise came, then disappeared only to return. The distraction teased him. The voices were childlike in screams and distant as if leaving shore on an invisible boat. He sat up and looked towards the source of this mild irritation. It was a party of people, mere specs on the far away point of the bay. Moving like disoriented ants, following their Queen trusting her path of adventure. His wind watering eyes smarted to distort his focus. The sight played its antics and confused him. He tried to count them but they were quite close and moving. Where on the island could they find such a small group of maybe four or five? There may have been more. There may have been fewer. But for all their momentary interest, they were causing little distraction to his purpose. He returned to his sketch pad opening it with a deep breath of sea air to clear his stray thoughts.

Time passed measured by his slow contented breathing. It was indeed a glorious day to work. The bright white pad begged for lead to make it less stark. Sam's hand wavered deciding where to resume his creation.

But the distant distraction would not dissipate voluntarily. Once more he glanced at the far away activity. He narrowed his eyes. Suddenly the truth emerged. It was so clear now. He realised the leader was his wife and the group were now huddled in discussion in a dune. He chuckled that it had taken so long for him to realise the blinking obvious. If it wasn't a school class, it would be Angie with her clients. What an inspirational venue, thought Sam. She was very much on top of her work and Sam smiled. He was proud of her, most of the time.

Then he noticed their sudden movement. They were dispersing and running towards the sea. All participated and splashed in the knee high cold Atlantic waves. Shouts increased in volume in the spume. Then Sam realised they were all naked. He remembered at last he had his binoculars in his bag. He took them out and focussed on the frolicking bodies in the water. Sure enough there was Angie splashing about in her birthday suit and being splashed by youngsters at various stages of puberty. That did not seem right. That might even be a source of official complaint by such a conservative native population. Sam felt anger unable to explode in his far-off solitude. His wife had gone too far this time. Of that he was in no doubt.

Of course she would have considered what she was doing, he thought, as his concentration centred on his broad pointed lead pencil once again. But he dismissed the offending images from his mind for the time being and returned to make his pad alive. He worked for almost another hour. Then the grassy banks bent over in unison. The charging clouds no longer white had an evil darkness to their contours, bringing a cool breeze. It was a further discomfort of the afternoon.

Sam took a deep sigh which terminated his work for the day, prematurely. The clouds were a warning forerunner. Rain was destructive for the out-of-door artist.

Rain could undo a painter's work in a moment of deluge. He felt a shiver. It was time to return home.

On arrival, outside his front door, was a box. It was narrow and looked heavy as it rested at an angle on the cottage wall and the loupin stane. He inspected its brown paper covering. In ink, with a smudged postal marking, was her name once more from a grateful parent.

Sam stirred the browning mince and kept an eye on the seething spaghetti. He consulted his watch. Any moment now.

'Hi, that's me back,' said Angie.

'Yeah .....good day?' asked Sam as usual.

'Sure. Got some good results this afternoon.'

'Hmmm...' he replied tapping the mince spoon firmly on the pan rim.

Angie came through to the kitchen and pecked Sam on his cheek.

'That smells good.'

'Yeah, fresh sea air builds up an appetite,' he said planning how to develop his themed interrogation.

'It certainly does,' she said.

'This afternoon...I was up on Keirfea...' he began.

'Tell me later, I'm going to change.'

♦

Forks spiralled round and round trapping the spaghetti before it made its cautious way to their mouths.

'As I was saying, up on Keirfea... I was drawing the bay.'

'Good day for it.'

'Yeah, good day for a swim too. Saw you all in the water.'

Angie's face lit up and she snorted a laugh.

'Yes, that's right. We went for a skinny dip. It was so refreshing,' she said.

'Bloody hell Angie. It's not what you did in Lancashire is it?'

'Hardly. No privacy on the beaches there.'

'Privacy? Not much privacy with all your clients in the buff,' he said raising his voice a notch.

'You should have joined us,' she teased.

'You must be crazy,' said Sam thumping his fist on the table making the salt and pepper pots vibrate.

'Why?'

'Because if it gets reported, you could be fired. Did you consider that?' Sam asked with indignation.

Angie laughed loudly. 'Get reported. Good idea. I should write an article in the British Psychological Society Journal. Cognitive Behaviour Therapy working wonders in the sea,' she said smiling at Sam.

'You don't get it do you? You can't justify what you want to do and call it work or therapy can you? You know there's still opposition to your centre here on the island? You are playing with fire Angie and I don't want you to get burnt.'

Angie turned away like a hurt dog. 'Don't be so angry, please. I knew what I was doing. If you saw us clearly you would have seen we were all female. All anorexic. To get them to see each other naked was important. It was an opportunity for each girl to think the others looked ill. Then realise they were the same, more underweight perhaps, even more ill. Perception is an important tool for a psychologist,' she said as if it was a university lecture.

Sam lowered his head and felt he had possibly misjudged his wife. 'That puts a slightly different shade on what I saw. But what if a local passing by saw you all?'

'I made sure no one was around and we were only in the water for a matter of minutes. Sam, therapy is a wide canvass,' said Angie drawing on Sam's professional territory.

Sam cooled off a little, a very little.

'Remember I mentioned that Edinburgh lad?'

'Yeah....Simon?'

'Yes, the elective mute. I was down with the boys on the beach earlier, in the morning...no not naked. Simon laughed and screamed in the water.'

'So would I. Bloody cold I imagine,' Sam said shaking his head.

'Invigorating you mean? Some of my clients have rarely seen the sea. Some are from high rise city flats with inadequate parents showing little interest in them. Give them new experiences. Give them control of their lives. Make them make their own decisions. That's what I'm doing. Sam, I do know what I'm doing, you know. It's how I cure some of them, that is if they are ready and want to be cured.'

'Maybe I just don't understand but I have a gut reaction and I think I probably share it with this community. Some things go beyond the pale. You are certainly a force to reckon with.'

'Results Sam. That's what I'm after. Results. That's what the families want. It's what the clients need too.'

'Hmmm..... we'll see. By the way there's a box for you, came today when I was out.'

'That sounds interesting. Let me see...it's well wrapped. Ahh a wooden box. Looks like a whisky. You'll like that,' she said.

'From another grateful admirer no doubt?' asked Sam in a sarcastic dirge of a voice.

'Yes, another very grateful admirer. McAllan premier single malt. Hmmmm...are you for a glass now?'

'Later perhaps. I'll wash up first.'

THREE

There were two bright-eyed students before her, not one. Angie looked perplexed at the papers on her desk, as if a letter to explain why she had acquired an extra placement would appear.

Clinical Psychology doctoral student Kevin P. Mensah was lanky, wore bright wine cords, large loafers and a striped coloured West African smock. He would not have looked out of place at any weed-scented 70's musical convention. He was, as his name suggested, also black. His final graduate year placement was from Glasgow University.

He arrived with Lucy Glass. She was petite and conventionally dressed in a high collared powder blue pullover, with an orange streaked silk scarf knotted loosely around her neck. Pierced ears showed a glint of a pearl. She wore a tight heavy clothed patchwork skirt, the sort frequently seen on trendy handbags. Her knitting needle legs were covered in warm heather-coloured woollen leggings. She was prepared for Orkney. Angie was not prepared for her.

'Goodness me. Two of you,' said the perplexed Angie.

The students looked at one another.

'I was certainly expecting Kevin. So where did you come from?'

Lucy searched in her bag diligently.

'I should have the introductory letter...somewhere in here....ummmm maybe I've forgotten it,' she said as she continued to fumble.

'So from which educational establishment have you sought sanctuary here on Orkney?'

'Er..a...Edinburgh.'

'I see...... Edinburgh ....would have been nice if they had informed me....but anyway two is always better than one, not so?' Angie replied seeing opportunities before her eyes.

'I thought they had notified you, Dr. Lawrence,' said Lucy.

'Not so unusual to have a missing letter sometimes, especially up here. Anyway, let's accept it was not your mistake. You are, presumably in your final year?'

'Yes, last placement,' said Kevin.

'So exams over? Results in?' asked Angie.

'Yes, passed. Viva too.'

'Good....and you, Lucy?'

'Sat and passed all except one or two re-sits, statistics my downfall really. But I am working on a third redraft of my thesis.'

'For you Kevin it's your doctorate if you pass this placement. Not so?'

'That's right,' he said revealing a bright white set of happy teeth breaking through a contented smile.

'A couple of fences to jump for you Lucy, but we'll get you on track here. No distractions as you can imagine.'

Lucy nodded politely with a smile. Dr Lawrence seemed to be favouring Kevin. No wonder. He seemed to have ticked all the boxes. Yet Lucy had surprised herself already. Somehow she had been taken on board. That was her first goal.

'We have a twelve bed assessment centre for youngsters between the ages of eleven and sixteen here.

Kids full of testosterone and others, well at times just bullshit, now developed into anorexia, bulimia and anxieties. There's a kitchen staff you will do well to keep on their side. They will fill you up with cakes all day if they could. There is one classroom with one teacher Mahrie Nicolson, a Lewis girl as you will hear. By the way if you think she's talking behind your back, she will be. It will be in Gaelic to her brother Callum, the chef. '

'I didn't know Gaelic was spoken on Orkney,' said Lucy.

'It's not. Callum and Mahrie come from Lewis, that's in the Hebrides,' said Angie showing her knowledge of the northern isles.

'Okay, I see,' said Kevin smiling at the thought of learning a new language already.

'Your accommodation will be at the end of the long corridor. Chose your rooms.'

Lucy noticed Kevin was already studying his centre brochure diligently, following Angie's descriptive narrative. Not having one, Lucy drew nearer to share the written information.

'Now you can eat breakfast and evening meals with the kids. That should keep your bank balances in order. So, go and familiarise yourselves with the building. Settle in and speak to anyone you want. They will want to know who you both are, especially you Kevin I imagine, you know, the African bit, so the sooner that process gets off the ground the better. Any questions?'

'No, understood,' said Kevin.

'Likewise,' said Lucy.

As the students left, Angie searched through the top layer of a three basket filing system. Then the middle one and lastly the bottom wire tray.

'Bloody hell. Two students,' she whispered under her breath. But try as she may, no introductory letter appeared for Lucy. 'Must tidy up here. Can't understand this,' she murmured.

'Tell them about Africa indeed,' said Kevin.

'Yes, what was that all about?' asked Lucy.

'I'm a third generation Glaswegian whose grandfather came from Ghana but he died before I was born. I've never been to Africa.'

♦

Sam was on the shore as still and as silent as a boat-yard crane. He was watching the movements of an active oyster catcher, the most improperly named bird he thought, as there was never any sight of an oyster being caught. He would be cooking them in garlic butter if they were as common. He relished the contrast to his years of urban life. Perhaps the movements of nature was a substitute for the crowds of people who froze on his city oil paintings. A flat stone with a marginal incline was chosen as his seat and soon he had laid out his instruments of art.

A collie barked. It ran towards the waves then retreated just as smartly. Its bark and wagging tail showed its enjoyment of the elements with no adversary in sight.

He saw the dog's master stroll casually kicking lengths of seaweed away in his path. He seemed to be a man of early seniority and one most certainly contented by life. His hair was grey, his face ruddy and weather beaten. He was supported by a gnarly but solid stick. As the minutes passed his presence grew nearer. Sam tapped his forehead acknowledging his presence.

'Mornin'. An artist, eh?'

'That's right. A great place to be an artist too.'

The man eyed him up and down, his collie circled the twosome.

'Yer a newcomer then?'

'Yes, six months ago.'

'So are you stayin?'

'More than ever. It was my wife's work that brought me here from Lancashire. But it has turned out just fine in my artistic career. A fresh start you know. I love it here, in all weathers,' said Sam ingratiating himself to the local.

'You'll not have seen the islands in the worst of weathers,' he said looking seaward, leaning on his walking stick. Sam saw National Trust visitor's stickers crookedly aligned down its knobbly length. They seemed weather-beaten and old.

'No not yet. A full force eight gale might get me out to photograph perhaps, from the shore of course. Too windy to draw,' said Sam.

'Aye and while you do that, I'm out there somewhere bringin' in the catch.'

'So you are a fisherman?'

'Aye, Harvest Store is my trawler. Three man crew. Both my sons and me.'

'And how is the fishing? Are they European quotas causing difficulty?' asked Sam.

'Naw, this is the herring season. They turn a blind eye tae that. They know it's around our Scottish shores in good summer supply.'

'Herring. The flashing silver herring?'

'So you know the fishing?'

'More the eating. A fresh herring is hard to beat.'

The man smiled with dancing eyebrows.

'They are only fresh if they are fried within five minutes of being caught.'

'You mean on board?'

'Aye, on board sir, that's what I mean.'

He strode forward and held out his hand.

'Sandy Flett.....the skipper.'

Sam moved his hips to reach his hand. The collie came up to lick the joining hands.

'Get away Blade.'

'Sam Lawrence,' he said stroking Blade's head as the hands parted.

'Lawrence....isn't that the name of the new psychologist woman at the new centre for the kids?'

'Yes, my wife Angie.'

'I see. ....so...how's the place doing, I mean after the opposition?'

'By the time we arrived the building was up and they needed cleaning, cooking and an occasional gardener and some auxiliary staff so there must have been some glad to see the project up and running.'

'Aye, it's the older folk. They don't understand the need for psychologists these days. Then there's the old, Not In My Backyard syndrome. I see where they are coming from mind you. I mean Rousay of all places. The folk your wife deals with are no locals, I'm sure of that. They won't understand the beat o' the land; the canny way we are up here. It's no city life, far from it.'

'I think that's seen as a benefit. I think this island is bringing something out in some children. They are gaining new experiences all the time.'

'Then tell yer wife this. I'll take them oot in the Harvest Store. An overnight run. Half way tae Norway, following the fish. That'll be a new experience fur them. Leave from Kirkwall at 5pm back at 7am the next day.'

'Some of the patients are female, you understand?' said Sam.

'Aye, that's nae a problem these days. They can wee in a tin can in the kludge on board, like us all. We're nae superstitious. So see if that fits with yer wife's understanding o' new experiences.'

'Sandy, I'm sure Angie will be interested in hearing this, yup I'm sure she will,' said Sam.

'Mind you it's no a pleasure craft. They'll have tae work too. Here, my card. Give me a ring one way or anaither,' the skipper said.

FOUR

Billy was a 15 year old truant. His voice had been late in breaking only the year before, a consequence of delayed maturation on account of his anorexia. He was not keen at first to be cast to the seas. His life had been cast to the winds so often. He had no confidence in sharing his views with the other teenagers. He was a Dundee boy who had seen the moods of the Tay, once so strong as to have downed the faulty Tay Bridge in 1879. He was the least enthusiastic of the clients to venture near the wild sea.

Despite all the weak anorexia cases, from which most of the girls suffered, there was mild enthusiasm for a trawler trip especially with the prospect of sighting Norway.

'I'll go too,' said Kevin.

'There you are girls. You will appreciate Kevin being there. What about you, Lucy? Are you seafaring?' asked Angie.

Lucy smiled with apologetic eyes. 'I'd be sea-sick. I just know it. I'll stay here.' Her words trailed away.

'Don't worry, I suspect we will have a few to care for at the centre.'

Lucy felt disappointed and wondered how she would be seen to have opted out so soon after the placement had started. With her unexpected arrival and now this, she felt in as much need of counselling as any of the resident youths. She sat with her legs tightly crossed and her hands clasped as if to make her small frame disappear.

'Can we meet to plan this trip?' asked Kevin.

'Excellent suggestion. Let's go to my office,' said Angie leading the way.

Lucy hesitated for a moment. She was really not part of this preparation. Kevin gave her an encouraging head nod and so the three sat down in Angie's room.

'Coffee?'

'Thanks Angie,' said Kevin.

'Yes coffee too, please. I'll make them.'

'Thanks Lucy. Now, this will be an overnight trip. Do you think that should cause any problems, Kevin?'

'No, as long as they don't remove their lifebelts,' he said.

'It's not their lifebelts I'd be more concerned about losing,' said Angie.

Kevin's academic mind could not gauge what Angie meant. He was soon enlightened.

'Their virginity Kevin, wakey wakey. They may be ill but there's testosterone around,' she said.

Kevin smiled. It was so obvious now.

'I don't think Elly should go. She's not ready, I don't think she'll cope. That's one for you Lucy,' said Angie.

'What do you expect they will get out of the trip?' asked Lucy stirring the coffees.

'Well, what do you think?'

'It will give them some confidence, a new experience; a feeling of achievement....'

'Exactly. These are children deprived of love, encouragement, of trust.'

'But how does that overcome and cure Anorexia?'

Angie hesitated. Lucy seemed almost naive, not doctorate material. She felt she would have much to improve if she wanted to make an impression.

'Lucy, no one can cure anorexia. There is no magic potion and hey presto....Mum give me a pizza. It doesn't work like that.'

'No. They say it's a three way split. One third recover in their own time and these are the ones that don't come here. Then there's the middle group,' said Kevin recalling his lectures.

'And that's very much our client list,' added Angie.

Kevin continued. 'Yes, they are. Some will make it after a while and some will deteriorate into the third group who succumb sadly through weakness and vulnerability of ailments.'

Angie nodded as Kevin spoke. 'In a nutshell, Kevin. So you see, that's the beauty of Rousay. We are the safety net for the middle group. They find a freedom they never had before. Domestic, imagined, and abusive pressures are suspended, not necessarily resolved. What we are doing is lighting tapers. One day some flicker of flame might just burn out the stubborn daemon of anorexia, bulimia, depression or hyperactivity that's lodged deep in their minds. But first and most pertinent of all, they need to want to change. No matter how small the steps, they must make progress on their own terms or we cannot provide any help.'

'I see. So it's a suck and see or bide our time period of care?' suggested Lucy.

Angie tried hard not to show her frustration.

'Lucy, there are two trite 'truisms' of childhood to remember. They are both equally, demonstrably, fallacious and false: that childhood is a 'carefree' time and that one's school days are the best days of one's life.'

Kevin reflected on Angie's wisdom. 'No two lives are ever the same, even within the same family. It makes the dynamics intriguing. I suppose wanting to understand the dynamics has made me a psychologist.'

'And we'll need psychologists more and more but here on Orkney you have a wonderful opportunity to close the text books and experiment. See what works. Note what works and record them,' said Angie.

'So who is coming with me on the fishing boat?' asked Kevin, changing the subject and atmosphere.

'There will be four patients. Troy, Sal, Nick and Mo. I'll come too,' said Angie.

'That makes six. I'll telephone the skipper and see when we can go,' said Kevin.

♦

Two days later the fishing boat Harvest Store left Kirkwall harbour sneaking out under the shadow of the transatlantic liners which fed their passengers to the gunnels then hired buses to take them to all the ancient historical sites before returning them on board for their six o'clock meal. The liners were despised by Orcadians. The tourists never got a chance to help the local economy.

The Harvest Store left in calm waters. Skipper Sandy Flett knew the swell would start soon, so got the passengers to work in their life-protector luminous jackets.

Ronnie, Sam's eldest son, was a seasoned sailor wearing a grey oatmeal knitted pullover and a navy tourie on his curly brown hair. He wore Doc Martin boots and on his left hand was a tattoo, a modest star and crescent moon. On his bare back was the bare front of Marilyn Munroe, or so he told the boys to their delight and imaginations.

His brother Alan was a man of few words. Known as the softest o' the family, he was a 'yes' man. He always wanted to please but he never knew how. That made him stare at people he had not met. They soon realised he was 'not quite all there' and so smiled their concern which he took as their happiness on seeing him. He giggled much. It was not that he saw humour in life, it was like a tic, an uncontrollable giggle which made others smile. That gave him his sense of worth, his enjoyment of life and much satisfaction. It even made the children laugh. Laughter was infectious. It also gave the children an insight into other forms of mental health. That was a lesson Angie was keen to promote on the debriefing back at the centre. But that would wait. Her night would require the eyes of a cat, the ears of the bat and the ringmaster's whip if needed.

'Gees a hand wi the tea,' requested Ronnie.

'Right Sal and Troy, off to the galley with Ronnie,' she said.

They made their way along the centre of the boat to the hatch and descended out of sight. Kevin shoved his hands inside his pockets and puffed out his cheeks.

'Feeling cold?' asked Angie.

'Not really. Just unaccustomed,' he said.

'Unaccustomed to.....?'

'Just the sea I suppose. My ancestors may have come here by sea but I guess they were the last of the family on the high seas. We're a family of land lubbers. I like my feet to be on solid ground.'

'Come on Kevin, set a good example or we'll all be swimming for shore,' said Angie.

'Don't worry, I'll cope.'

Black smoke left the funnel steaming out like a banshee on the run. Diesel fumes sought out the nostrils of the children and they showed its disapproval. Alan knew what action would distract them from their misery.

'Take the line,' said Alan.

'Nick, Mo, do what Alan is asking,' Angie said.

Nick moved slowly to Alan unsure of him.

'Throw the line overboard. You, Mo, bring that wooden box over here,' insisted Alan.

'Nick bring the line in again.'

'Why? Did I not do it right?'

'No, you'll have caught some mackerel,' said Alan clapping his hands and giggling once more.

Sure to his word the dark green backed striped fish leapt on board with regularity. Many were freed from their hook and slithered around amongst wary legs.

'Pick up the stray fish and put them in the box dearie,' said Alan.

Mo picked up a mackerel by its tail. It squirmed, and shook itself free.

'It won't bite it's not a shark,' Alan reminded her.

'I can't touch them. There're slimy,' said Mo.

Alan brought a wide brushless broom for Mo to eke out the stray fish and send them down the fore hatch into the boxes now being attended by Sandy, the skipper. When the lines were in, a welcome voice was heard.

'Tea's up,' shouted Ronnie twice.

'I don't need any,' said Mo.

'Come on lass, it will warm you up,' suggested Sandy but his paternal advice was rejected by the sustenance avoiding anorexic.

The crew and passengers sat down in the cabin with their teas. They sat shoulder to shoulder.

'Eugh, that tastes horrible,' said Nick pushing his mug away.

'You're right, just shitty,' said Mo who pretended to sup her cup.

Alan laughed and giggled.

'It's not funny. I'm not drinking that,' said Sal who then pushed her mug away.

'Easy now. It's okay. What you are not used to is the condensed milk. You see we can't get fresh milk when we're at sea for a long time. Nae fridge. So we use canned condensed milk. That's what it is,' said Ronnie.

'Have a Glengarry biscuit with it. You'll soon get used to it. An' if you usually take sugar with your tea, don't. The condensed milk is sweet enough. C'mon dearie take a biscuit, it'll calm yer stomach I tell ye,' encouraged Sam.

Angie watched as anorexic Sal took one biscuit. Sea air and spray was having a curative impact.

Alan went round everyone a minute later as some were eating their biscuits and offered another one while still in a state of giggles. Soon his mirth was echoed by Troy and Nick. Then Sal and Mo started to giggle and the infection remained with them awhile but no more biscuits were taken.

When the atmosphere settled Sal was the first to go up on deck followed by Nick and Mo. By the time Angie and Kevin were on deck, it was too late. All three had poked their fingers to the back of their throats and made themselves sick. Sickness lay on the deck moving slowly one way then another. Feet danced to avoid its progress on the deck.

'Ok, stand back,' called Ronnie holding a hose and clearing the deck of the pungent smell in a swift cleansing arc. He then squished some pine scented toilet liquid over the offending area and again the hose dispatched the resultant froth. Moments later the deck was as clean as new and the air, sea-salted of course, also had an out-of-place pine, scent to delight observing nostrils.

'It was the tea. Too sickly for me,' said Troy.

'Rubbish it's coz we're anorexic,' said Nick.

'No I'm not, ya bastard,' shouted Troy.

Before another word was said the two boys started to grapple. They lost their footing easily and landed on the deck tearing each other's eyes out.

'For goodness sake boys. Stop it', called Angie. They paid no attention.

Kevin tried to separate them but they clung to each other like limpets, flailing fists and feet.

'Stand back, stand back,' shouted Alan who approached with the sea water bearing hose.

Alan aimed at their backsides and saw them move around the deck at his beck and call. As he eventually separated them his nervous giggle grew louder.

'That's enough Alan. Now you two get down below and get dried. You could have ended up in the North Sea. Bear that in mind,' said Angie.

Angie turned to Kevin on the deck.

'Phew that was a risky incident. Hard to explain to parents their son was accidentally washed overboard. Drowned at sea. I don't think it's a scenario I could face.'

'Well fortunately it was not as bad as that and taking risks is what this game is all about,' Kevin replied walking to the bow of the boat. Angie followed holding on to anything that she could reach. A coil of tarred jute rope lay at the bow offering a solid perch for them. They sat in close proximity.

'You are twenty eight aren't you Kevin?'

'Yes, why?'

'Just wondering.'

'Wondering what? That I'm not married?'

'No, wondering how old Lucy is. I think she's much younger but I could be wrong.'

'She's only twenty two. She told me,' said Kevin.

'Hmmm twenty-two, I see. That probably explains it. A lack of confidence perhaps. A lack of knowledge too. But I think the placement will be good for her. Positive experiences are so crucial, Kevin, aren't they?'

Kevin smiled showing his bright white teeth against the tinkling sky. 'If you say so, they are.'

'But they are Kevin, they are.'

'Okay I hear you. Yes, of course they are. I was just wondering what you will think up next.'

'That's easy. I think an hour's rest before we are called to work again. Let's get back down and see what's happening.'

Kevin held his hand out to support Angie. As she rose their heads drew closer together. Angie instinctively and unprofessionally gave Kevin a peck on his cheek. He turned away. He let go of her hand. She took the rail and held it firmly as they slithered along the deck to the hatch. Neither commented on the fleeting gesture but it played on their minds longer than each other thought.

♦

While the others remained at sea, Lucy had three residents to supervise but all were in their beds when she entered Angie's office. She put the light on. Then she closed the blinds. She looked along the row of books in Angie's glass bookcase. Impressive. Most were professional psychology books but author Lee Child seemed to dominate the middle shelves. Lucy contemplated the subject matter. Killing Floor; Bad Luck & Trouble; Tripwire; Die Trying. She reflected on the hard boiled and commercial style of Child's writing as she had read many of the Jack Reacher series by this author. Pretty hard hitting reading she thought. Did that meet one of her needs? Then she saw a collection of works on the same theme in an embossed folder. She took that one down from the shelf. She noticed Angela was the author of this document on Post Traumatic Stress Disorder. It was her doctoral thesis from Glasgow University.

In the cupboard beneath, Lucy found a folder bound by an elastic band. She took it off. There were many stapled papers in the bulky document. There were different thicknesses of papers. But all seemed to have one subject matter. A topic not mentioned on the folder cover. It was the largely untreatable Anti Social Personality Disorder. Lucy wondered why there was so much information on this rather rare and largely untreatable condition.

Then a sneeze made its way to her detective eyes. Her paper hanky accepted the nasal explosion. She threw the screwed up tissue into the wastepaper basket. Then she thought that would confirm she had been loitering in Angie's office so she retracted it. In doing so, she disturbed the other items previously jettisoned into the receptacle. One gave a glint of silver. It was an empty strip of pills. She examined the blister pack carefully. She read through the punctured pill covers. 100mg Lamotrigine tabs. Take one twice daily.

Lucy knew from her father's daily medication that Lamotrigine served two purposes. It was used to lessen epilepsy attacks. She was familiar with that condition. There had never been any sign or admission of that problem in her supervisor. The other ailment it addressed was for Bi-Polar conditions. Did that make her mood swings favour Kevin over her? Or was she being over sensitive? She placed the blister pack back in the wastepaper basket. She turned off the light and opened the curtains. A nocturnal bat flashed by outside. Lucy gasped and emitted a soft high squeal. For a moment she felt her espionage had been detected.

FIVE

Light was star provided. The sky cloudy in part and dark as a dinner suit elsewhere. The swell was manageable but not comfortable for land folk. The boat's entire compliment stood on the deck holding on to any immobile fixture. They watched as the nets were thrown overboard.

'Stand aside. Keep off the net or you'll be thrown into the sea,' warned Skipper Sandy.

The orange and the yellow balls secured to the net were launched and settled on the water. Then as they drifted away from the boat, they disappeared out of sight like snow on a warm car bonnet. It took another ten minutes to launch all the nets.

'Right, down below, all of ye,' said the skipper.

The children sat with Kevin and Angie in a circle around the floor-fixed wooden table with a retaining lip. Sandy sat on a top bunk, his shoe-less legs dangling. In his hands was a medium sized accordion and he began to play and sing. Alan gave everyone an ice lolly from a box freezer and instructed everyone to eat it quickly so that with the sticks, they would play a game. Troy didn't seem interested. He looked quite glum.

'It will be good for settling your tum, Troy,' said Kevin.

Then he opened his lolly and licked slowly.

Mo opened her wrapper and looked for a convenient

place to discard the lolly. Alan saw her think this way. His perception was spot on.

'We need all the lollies to get the sticks so get sucking the ices. I'm counting on you all.'

Angie was pleased to see Mo start to lick her lolly.

Troy dropped his ice. 'Oh god no. It's fallen on the floor. I can't eat it now,' he said hiding his triumphant deception.

'Here, give it to me. I'll wash it,' said Sandy. He did so and returned it to a disappointed Troy. But Troy was consoled that the washing process would have made the lolly smaller.

Ice-lollies dripped in the stuffy warmth of the hold.

'Quick sook up the lolly,' shouted the giggling Alan.

Angie and Kevin turned their lollies around to catch the juice which in turn, coloured their tongues.

'Look at your yellow tongue, Angie,' laughed Troy.

'Yours is bright cherry Kevin,' Angie commented.

Alan pointed at all the coloured tongues and giggled. It was enough encouragement for all the patients to lick their melting lollies, colour their tongues and retain their sticks.

'Noo, let's play Shove Halfpenny. But here it's shove sixpence. We've nae halfpennies nae mair,' said Ronnie setting up goals at each end of the table. 'Four teams o' two. Call yourself whatever team ye wish and let's play.'

So Arbroath v Rangers; Hibs v Chelsea; Partick Thistle v Arsenal and Morton v Manchester United played for over an hour as the lollipop sticks flashed and the sixpence flew around the table. And for all this time Sandy ran his fingers up the vertical accordion keyboard on one hand and seemingly with a wandering hand selected the buttons by the other. It was good to see the children laugh and smile and Alan kept the score, although rather badly.

'No it's us, Morton, that got the goal. Not Man United,' said Troy indignantly. Alan amended the score on the slate he marked up in chalk and giggled.

It seemed that Troy and Nick had patched up their differences and the game which seemed new to all of them, turned out to be a great success.

Around 11.30pm, the yawns were increasing. Sandy secured his instrument, came down from his perch and showed every one which bunk they were sleeping in. The children clambered in fully clothed, save for their footwear. The warm oily engine fumes acted like an illegal high and soon the children were sleeping soundly.

'Shall we star gaze?' asked Angie.

Kevin looked at the skipper, hoping the request was directed at him.

'Aye, up ye go but keep a firm grip. I'll be in the wheel house till Ronnie takes over. We'll keep an eye oot on you so ye dinnie fall overboard,' said the Skipper.

Angie put her shoes on again and mounted the few step to the deck. Kevin followed reassured that the captain would keep an eye on them. They returned to the rear of the ship where the coiled rope had vanished. Kevin lifted a box and stood it on its end. His hand invited Angie to sit. He stood beside her with his back supported by a vertical wooden pole.

'You are certainly a different type of supervisor, if you don't mind me saying,' he began.

'How many have you had?'

'Let me see. Not till the second year...that's four I've had, making you the fifth.'

'And so how do I compare?' she asked looking out to the dark inky sea and starry sky.

'I guess you are less hung up. Less formal. Mind you being up here makes that a different placement, I suppose. Yet even if you were in the city, I'm sure you'd be the same.'

'A leopard can't change its spots then,' she said.

'I suppose not. Your husband Sam. He's an artist. Artist - Psychologist. That's a strange combination, isn't it?' asked Kevin.

'Healthier than two artists or two psychologists marrying each other.'

'I suppose so. Can I ask how you met each other?'

'You mean was it love at first sight?'

'Well, was it?'

'I had completed my thesis at Glasgow and took a London holiday. I had never been out of Scotland. But I didn't have much money in those days. I saw as many of the tourist sites I could. Then I went to Manchester for a few weeks. Seeing the sites and some office jobs in the daytime. Then I saw a card in the window. That's where I met Sam.'

'In Manchester?'

'Manchester Art School. As I said money was short in my life. They paid well for life study models for the artists. I spent a week doing that. One of the artists was Sam.'

Kevin laughed. 'You mean when Sam first set eyes on you, you were a nude model?'

Angie laughed. 'The things we do when we are young.'

'No regrets?'

'You should visit our small loo. That's where he hung that picture of me as his model. He captured my youth. I'll be forever young.'

'So that's your Manchester connection?'

'Yes, two years later, a small wedding in a registrar's office. Not what I had always dreamt of, of course. I got my first clinical psychology job there at the Royal Children's hospital while Sam painted. He made quite a name for himself. I sometimes wonder if he made the right decision heading for Orkney. He says it's fine though.'

'I've seen some of his seascapes. I think they're brilliant.'

'Yes, they are good. But he's losing out on some of the connections which artists have. I am sure.'

'Aren't they all on e-mail these days?'

'Oh no Kevin. Art people are feely-touch folk. They need to communicate with their eyes and hands, not their stationary keyboards.'

'So what got you into clinical psychology in the first place? Did it run in the family?'

'No....I'm getting cold. Let's get into our bunks down below.

♦

A bell rang throughout the boat. It was 3am.

'Time to collect the creels. Com'on now, this will be worth seeing,' said Ronnie.

Slowly each youngster appeared from below coming up the hatch. The bright lights on deck made them shade their eyes. Yawns and groans were their only communication. On deck boxes had been packed one on top of the other.

'We're about twenty miles off Stavanger,' said the Skipper.

'Off where?' asked Sal.

'Off Norway. Where the Vikings come from. Look over there, see these lights on the shore? That's Norway,' replied Ronnie.

On hearing this, the children became excited asking Sandy to land on Norway.

'We've no passports. We'd get arrested.'

'We could sell them fish,' suggested Troy.

Alan laughed. 'Norwegians fish for themselves.'

Round the capstan the tarred rope coiled, dragging in the heavy line. It did so slowly.

'Perhaps it's got seaweed caught in it,' suggested an interested Nick.

'That's a good sign. No not seaweed.Just wait and see,' said the Skipper.

Sure to his word a creel tipped over into the boat and two adult lobsters with hands the size of a heavy weight boxer and as sharp as pinking shears moved over each other. Alan opened the creel and took one of them out. He showed it to the youngsters. They let out a sea monster howl. Alan tied the main claws together and placed them in a covered box.

Another creel surfaced and within the next hour eight more creels. The smaller lobsters were thrown back into the sea but sixteen of the armoured snappers were in the wooden boxes with a weight on top. They would be flown from Kirkwall to London in a few hours time and be on some London Menu that night.

'Now don't you be going to sleep again. The shrimps will be ready to collect in an hour,' warned the Skipper.

Only forty minutes later the smaller creels were being raised from the sea bed. They were landing in droves. Alan stopped to take one out. He broke its back. Flipped it open and ate the soft creamy flesh.

'Hmmmmm lovely....' he giggled. 'Anyone want a fresh shrimp to taste?'

Troy put his hand up.

'Here, take the flesh out,' he said after breaking the shrimp open. 'You like it?'

'Yea. Can I have another?'

'Ok just one more, 'Alan said.

Sal then Mo took their turn and ate the shrimps. But Nick said he didn't like fish. Angie was disappointed but pleased so many of the other anorexic cases did eat until she saw Mo head to the other side of the boat. She followed in time to see her cupping her hand from her mouth and throwing the un-chewed shrimp back to its home, unshelled. It would not survive long. It was now hookless bait for a hungry fish.

Not long after they returned to their bunks, the wind started to freshen and the waves grew. The bobbing boat's progress was slowed and one by one the sick bags appeared. First to use hers was Angie. Nik and Sal began to cry. Not a loud cry but a sobbing. The source was clear. An unearthly hour, a lack of sleep and a rollicking boat. It was a miserable concoction.

Alan moved around distributing new sick bags while gathering the used ones. It was far from the most pleasant of jobs but he did so with his inimitable giggle.

They were all sick except Nick who had refused his fishy tit bits, and of course the regular crew who were used to rough seas. It was however a disappointment for Angie once more to see all the lobster and shrimp re-appear from her anorexic patients' stomachs.

There were cries and no comforting could address the constant motion of the boat bobbing up and down.

'Another three hours and we'll be back in Kirkwall,' the skipper said.

'Three hours. I'll not live that long,' said Troy.

'Try and get some sleep, all of you,' said Kevin.

'Good idea. That'll make time pass quickly,' said Angie smiling at Kevin whose eyes were already closed.

◆

As the church clock chimed 9am the Harvest Store was in sight of the town.

'Home at bloody last,' said Nick.

'Did you not enjoy it?' asked Alan.

'It was all right at the start but after that...euch...I'm not going to be a sailor,' Nick said making a face etched with disgust.

'I'm not a sailor. I'm a fisherman,' laughed Alan before his giggles started again.

SIX

Edinburgh High Court
25th November 1988

Tony Arnold's bones were shaking as the Black Maria approached the High Court on the shining wet cobbled stones of Auld Reekie, Edinburgh. Fear was the main cause. Tony was a confused man whose demeanour showed some level of sorrow. But there was only one sentence his Lordship could give.

Part of the murder evidence had been given to the Jury by his six year old daughter. She spoke of times when her mother was out late. She said she used heavy makeup on her face often. Then she said she loved her parents but didn't know why her father killed her mother. Then she began to cry profusely. The Judge directed the child to be excused from court.

The Jury had considered the evidence and found Tony Arnold guilty of killing his wife in a sober, planned and fatal blow to the skull. His Lordship had requested a background report prior to sentencing. Not a normal procedure in a murder verdict but his Lordship was inquisitive. He wished to make sense of this senseless murder, see what kind of animal was before him and adopt the appropriate manner in which to deliver the sentence.

Handcuffs were unlocked when Tony arrived at the dock in a smart tieless cream shirt and brown suit. His black greasy hair had avoided a comb that morning as if the sentencing appointment had disturbed his sleep. Two large sombre security guards stood on either side of him and a uniformed policeman was near at hand should anything untoward happen.

Tony stood when told to but his gaze was to compare his High Court appearance with the numerous televised episodes of Cracker court appearances. He was aware the tariffs were stark in this setting. He wished the stage fright procedure was over soon. It wasn't the inevitable life sentence Lord McEwan would deliver which concerned Tony. The question now at the front of his mind was how long was life according to Lord McEwan?

◆

Three days later at the instigation of the Social Work Department in Kilmarnock, Sheriff Sheila McCulloch freed for adoption seven month old Mark, of the imprisoned Tony and the late Mrs Margaret Arnold. The six year old daughter, Angelina Arnold, was deemed to be too old for adoption and was sent into the care of the local authority. From that day, her home was at the Firbank Children's Home in Elderslie, Renfrewshire.

SEVEN

It was raining. It seemed Sunday was always wet to dampen her day-off for Angie. She listened half-heartedly to Desert Island Discs to the musical choices of some industrialist who had been knighted a decade ago. His music was staid; too classical; not enough variety. It was a knock on the door which terminated her listening. She strode towards the door in her slippers and dressing gown. In her mind it was probably a rumpus or fight in the centre that she was about to have reported to her.

When the door opened Angie stood fixed staring at the blue suited man of around fifty years of age. He wore a tie and his shoes were polished black. On one hand was a drooping plastic bag and on the other a dog. A Bassett hound in fact.

'Good morning. You are the manager of the Assessment centre?'

'Well yes. Can I help you?'

'I am Angus McFadden. Born and bred in Kirkwall but long since gone from the island. I was wondering rather, if I can help you?' he said as the hound looked up at Angie with soulful eyes.

'Come in. I am interested to hear what you have in mind.'

'Sam, a visitor. Two in fact.'

'Coming, be with you soon,' he replied from the far end of the house as he wiped away sleep from his eyes and stretched.

'Do have a seat. Oh, I seem to have given your dog a command,' said Angie as the hound beat his master to the sofa.

'Down Arthur!' The dog flopped down from the soft seat. 'He appreciates any command. But he chooses which ones to obey. To get to the bottom of this visit, I should say I like your work here on the island,' he began.

'You know what we do here?'

'No, I don't really. I live in London, where I have a house in Fulham. It was my mother at Kirkwall that told me about your establishment. But she's had a stroke, a major one down both sides. So I came up to arrange for her care at a residential home in Aberdeen. And of course to put her home on the market.'

'I see. I'm sorry to hear that.'

'Thank you. So that's our last generation on the island gone. Except Arthur.'

'So this is Arthur?' asked Sam entering the lounge and making straight to the dog, rubbing his pendular ears.

'Yes, Arthur is my problem and I was wondering if he could be your colleague at the centre?'

Angie smarted for a moment. More like offloading a dog seemed to be Angie's assessment. But she was also thinking out of the box.

'You mean permanently? You are donating Arthur to us?'

'I know I sound like a slave trader but Arthur is very amenable. In fact he can never get enough loving,' Angus said with eyes as droopy as his canine companion.

'Well I certainly think he'd be appreciated at the centre. I think it's a very generous donation. Yes, we'd love to have him, won't we Sam?'

'Er...will it be a centre dog or one who lives with us?' asked Sam.

'He's just like me. Can't get enough love. He can

have two homes,' suggested Angie.

'But he is a Bassett hound. You know what you are taking on board?' asked Angus.

'Four small legs, a long body, outsized ears and a tail, not so?' suggested Angie.

'That's outside. I meant what goes on in his head. He's calm, affectionate...'

'Ideal,' said Angie.

'Yes but also self-willed and disobedient at times,' said Angus.

'Absolutely perfect. Should go down a treat with the clients.'

'Make sure you don't leave any food around. He's a better vacuum cleaner than the electrical sort. And when I say food, especially food on the table unguarded, beware,' said Angus.

'Sadly not a temptation for some of our clients. But I'm coming round to the idea. It will be a challenge, for someone like me who has never had a dog to look after, but we're up for it aren't we Sam?'

'Over to you, I'll be out painting most of the day,' he replied.

'I am sure you are going to have a great life here Arthur,' said Angus standing up.

'He doesn't seem upset at your leaving,' said Sam surprised.

'Well, he's never been my dog. He's only eighteen months old and was of course my mother's pride and joy. I only met him twice before.'

'And your bag. Is that his feed?' asked Sam

'Yes, water bowl, a feeding bowl and a packet of his food. Once a day, two handfuls of the mixture with some water to mix it. Mind you he'll find food throughout the day if you are not careful.'

Sam realised the man had repeated himself. That this

was a canine industrial cleaner was no longer in doubt.

Arthur lay his bones down noisily and ignored Angus's departure. His ears spread out on the carpet. His nose sniffing the air while his dilated pupils wondered where the crumbs might be. He gave out a loud canine groan and then a rather unpleasant fart. He was already at home.

◆

Two weeks later, after Arthur had settled into the centre, where all fell in love with this canine carcass of undying love, Angie took a trip to Kirkwall.

She took the car over with her and filled her boot with provisions of both edible and domestic purchases. Then she walked down to Junction road where she found Petmania, an established pet shop of over thirty years in the town. It catered for every pet owner's requirements.

Angie bought Arthur's dog food in a large heavy strong paper bag. As she opened her purse, she noticed some local adverts selling sheep dogs and others offering ewes. One card caught her notice.

'How old is the parrot for sale?'

'You should never ask a parrot its age. They live for almost eighty years but this one arrived unexpectedly. A ship called into the harbour and sold it to us. We think it might be around ten years old. Just a youngster,' said Annie Gow.

'But it might be seventy nine and before long I'd have a dead parrot. You know a not-living, extinct, deceased, parrot,' Angela remarked with a mischievous smile.

Annie laughed. 'They are real chatter boxes. If you say something too often it will come to haunt you.'

Angie thought to herself how a parrot could be taught, by her clients. It was worth considering. A psychology assistant paid in nuts. Now that was a first she thought.

'So how much is the parrot?'

'Have you ever had a caged bird before?'

'Yes we had a caged budgerigar where I lived when I was young.'

'But I bet it was your parents who cleaned the cage each week,' she said innocently.

Angie smiled and simply said, 'Probably.'

'Hmmm...this one will need a sturdy cage. And a stand. But for stand, a bag of nuts, a secure cage and the African Grey, that will cost £450. I'll give you the lot for £410.'

'I'll pay by card, if I may.'

◆

'What, a parrot?' Sam's hands held his head in a tortured grip. 'For God's sake Angie. No discussion. You just go out and buy a bloody parrot.'

'An African Grey in fact. Isn't he handsome?'

'My God, whatever next. If a snake charmer rang the bell would you take a cobra too?'

'Oh Sam, don't be so silly. Both Arthur and ..er... oh..I've not given it a name yet,' she remarked scratching her head. 'Anyway don't worry, I'll get the kids to select a name. Good practice for them to make suggestions and decisions.'

'It's going to take some time getting used to these newcomers, I warn you,' he said.

'Oh not really. Arthur has taken to you. You can't deny it, Sam.'

'Thanks a million. Arthur will endear himself to everyone including the bin man.'

'Especially the bin man, I think,' said Angie.

'Exactly. Doesn't that teach us something?' he said not quite sure what conclusion he had actually reached himself, so he avoided eye contact.

Sam considered the consequences of this all-of-a-sudden animal behaviourist psychologist of a wife. She had a point, of course she always did, although he was still not sure what it was. Safer to drop the matter. See how the parrot might settle at the centre. He'd reserve judgement.

'You want a cuppa?' he asked.

The parrot turned its neck to listen to Sam. He seemed to be interested in what he was saying already, or was it internalising a fading Lancastrian accent?

EIGHT

The parrot was now named by popular demand Harry after Harry Styles of One Direction. And Harry soon identified with his new status in the centre.

'Hello Harry. I'm Harry.'

Talking to himself amused the children but with such an interest being made of the caged bird, his vocabulary soon expanded.

'Don't eat that crap.'

'Ohhh ....Fuck.'

It was such an explosive 'Fuck' that Angie began to have worries about this impulsive purchase. Ground rules had to be set.

1. No teaching Harry any swearing.
2. Harry was to be a friend and so no bad language or mistreatment would be allowed.
3. If the rules were not adhered to, then Harry would be sold.

Angie felt confident that the rules would not be breached. But perhaps she had missed out one rule.

Harry blotted its cage once more. In the dining room as plates where being slopped down and cutlery crashing into the dish washer, Harry had begun to sing.

'Mo is a fart and Sam does art. Mo is a fart and Sam does art.'

It was a comment which could have been lost in the mayhem of surreptitious plate scraping but Mo heard and the matter was reported to Angie. Of course no one owned up to teaching the parrot to offending Mo but the damage was done and offended she rightly was. Furthermore unlike a camera with a delete button, Harry's line was embedded in his memory. That was a worry.

Angie did not of course mind any neutral remark about her husband but personal abuse by children was not on. She began a series of individual interviews. To her room she called each client one by one. It was a private and confidential meeting with only three present. Arthur was the third and crucially silent member. Harry was excluded.

Troy was twelve years of age. A native of inner Glasgow; his mother died of foetal alcohol syndrome not long after he was born so he was brought up by an aunt who found his truancy then thefts, drug taking and general behaviour beyond her control. This lifestyle had also led to eating disorders for him.

'So Troy. Tell me how you are feeling?'

'Fine,' he said.

'Ok. Fine to go home? Fine to being here; fine because you are doing well at class?'

'Yea. I like it here. There's no pressure. I can concentrate in class, so I can.'

'No pressure. Really?' asked Angie.

'I don't know. Perhaps it's just because the class is small.'

'Well in a small class and you can cope. You are not in a city gang; you are in the wilderness here. You are managing Troy. You are doing well. What do you like most?'

'Arthur. I've taken him for walks and he's been in my room at night. He's great.'

'That's good Troy. Can you keep it up?

'I want to.'

'That comment about Mo. Did you know anything about it?'

Troy fidgeted as he denied anything about the remark.

'Troy I hear what you are saying, clearly, but your body language tells me something different. It tells me you are angry with me for asking. Now why would that be you think? Take a moment to think Troy.'

Troy took a moment, observed in his deepening blush and now sitting on his hands.

'Ok but I didn't think Harry would repeat it. Honest.'

'A parrot can be like a tape recorder Troy. Teach it to talk or sing but you know the rules now. Understand?'

Troy was quick to agree he understood and felt he was getting off lightly.

'You did not mean what you said about Mo, did you?'

''No. Of course not.'

'Then tell her. Go and apologise. Okay?'

But before Troy could conclude the interview, there was a knock on the door.

'Ok Troy that's all just now. Back to class,' said Angie heading for the door. Troy left looking up at the tall men standing there.

'Dr Lawrence?' asked the plain clothed policeman.

'Yes.'

'May we come in? We have a few questions for you.'

♦

That evening Angie was quieter than usual.

'You Ok?' asked Sam after their evening meal. 'Feeling under the weather?'

Angie approached Sam. 'No darling. Just reflecting on my childhood.'

♦

The following day it was Simon's turn. The elective mute sat beside Angie as she recalled his recent behaviour in the sea.

'You remember when we went swimming that morning? You liked that didn't you?'

'Mmmh.....' he said.

'The water was cold and it gave you a shock. It gave us all a shock, the water was freezing.'

Angie wrapped her arms around herself then shook them by her side as she had done when they paddled. 'And I hear you have been talking to Harry? Is that right?'

'Yes.'

'Have you taught him any new words?'

'Yes' Simon smiled.

'Which words have you taught Harry?'

Simon giggled.

'Was it I support Dundee Utd?' asked Angie.

His smile grew larger. He nodded.

'You have been trying hard Simon. I think you should have a special time with Harry. Just you and him. Would that be good? Is that what you want?'

'Yes please, I'd like that,' the elective mute said.

♦

Angie's next interview was for Mo. Her parents had been killed in a car crash on the M7 and as a five year old, an aunt and uncle cared for her. But they had their own children and Mo, as the youngest, felt marginalized. She did not fit in that Larbert home. Truancy and drug taking had taken its hold and until she confronted the reality of her parent's untimely death, *Thanatos,* that invisible death wish, had entered her mind and her weight suffered dramatically. It was no use telling her she was once a beautiful girl and still was. It was not how she wanted to be. Mo was anorexic and was in extensive bed rest. She entered the room with Arthur.

'Did you have a dog at home Mo?'

'No.'

'You like Arthur and Harry?'

'Not Harry,' she said.

'Has Troy apologised to you?'

'Yes.'

'Did he say it nicely?'

Mo raised her head a fraction and smiled with slightly parted lips.

'So you prefer Arthur?'

'Hmmm ..I really love them both. Arthur's nicer to touch.'

'He also needs walks. Would you like to walk him?'

Mo hesitated. She knew how this interview was going. She turned in towards herself, looking down.

'He needs lots of walks. He likes to smell the ground. He's a hound after all,' reminded Angie.

'But you won't let me walk him will you?'

'I want you to walk him but you know what you'll have to do?' smiled Angie stroking her hair as she did so. 'It's going to take some time but that should be what to aim for. Sorry Mo, your weight is lower than I'd like it to be, much lower.'

'If I eat a banana tonight can I walk him?'

Angie shook her head. She took her arm and stroked it gently. Fine hairs grew on her arms. It was a sign of great weight loss.

'Mo, I'm sorry. You need to go back to hospital. I'll arrange your transport.'

'No, that means force feeding,' she said with all the power her frail voice could muster.

'We want you to live Mo, to stay alive. It's your turn to help yourself. Time to think how you can walk Arthur.'

◆

When the air ambulance arrived on flat turf near the Centre, the whole school were out to support Mo. Lucy made a cordon of rope with Kevin at one end. Arthur sniffed around the helicopter looking for its entrance. Mo was brought out on a stretcher to cheers of good wishes and clapping. Angie bent down and lifted Arthur. She brought him to the prostrate girl. Mo touched his nozzle then stroked his big ears. Arthur tried to lick her but Angie held him back.

'I'll be back Arthur,' she said.

'Yes, we hope so soon Mo. Give it a real go. Work your way back to us,' said Angie.

◆

Sam was at home when the postman called.

'One to sign for your wife,' Mr Lawrence.

Sam looked at the official letter. It was franked from Glasgow, the Procurator Fiscal service, Crown Office, no less. He signed the registered letter.

'And the box. No need to sign,' he said.

Sam took the box and gave it a shake. He saw the postmark was Glasgow. That convinced him.

'Here, you have it. It's a box of chocolates,' Sam said handing the box back to the postman.

'How do you know? I couldn't tell,' the bewildered postman replied.

'If I'm wrong, then bring it back but if it's chocolates, eat them up. I'm pretty sure I can tell,' said Sam turning towards the front door.

'Well, thank you very much. Very kind of you.'

'By the way, are you married?' asked Sam turning back.

'Yes, married with three kids.'

'Stick around. I'll have flowers for you to give to your wife soon.'

Sam was satisfied he had breached the flow of gifts and looked forward to giving the postman and his family unexpected presents. That would slow down Angie's grateful benefactors. He wondered if she would notice.

NINE

Glasgow High Court
27 the March 2015

Angela had not been in Glasgow for a number of years. It still had its chattering jokers; its orange and green tribal busses and its joi de vivre in contrast to the Capital's volcanic solemnity. She walked between the towering Victorian buildings and felt small. She made her way past offices as her heart beat increasingly louder in her mind. It was a mind that flashed through her life's high and lows. There had been many more recent highs but this day was about the lows and she wondered if she had dressed appropriately for a nervous professional. She looked at her watch. She had just enough time for a quick coffee at the café she was passing to heighten her senses, so instinctively entered and went to the counter to ask for a Café Latte with extra sugar.

'You know there's a shot of syrup in this one?' asked the olive skinned dark haired smiling Italian server.

'Two sugars, please.'

'Okay, madam,' he said depressing the steaming hot milk. 'Anything else? A blueberry bun, fresh sultana scones?'

'No, just the coffee, thanks.'

'That's £2.75 then.'

Angie opened her purse and noticed her fingers shake. She sorted her change and thrust £3 on to the glass counter. 'Keep the change.'

'Thank you. I'll bring it to your table.'

Angie took a table facing the street and contrasted her life on Orkney with the stream of determined city walkers. It was an unfamiliar pace despite having been less than a year away from Manchester. Now her life events of her childhood seemed out of sequence. Could she retrieve them in an ordered fashion?

She was oblivious to the coffee's arrival.

'There you are,' said the server.

Angie turned anxiously to the waiter with an anxious gaze before looking at the creamy coffee and thanking him. She placed both her hands round the glass beverage stoically suffering the burning hot liquid for longer than was comfortable. It was pain she was recalling but could she change it into words?

She sipped until the latte descended half way down the mug. Then she made for the ladies, where she took out her powder puff and dabbed her cheeks. She looked at the peach lipstick half hidden in her purse and decided to lightly apply a minimal amount. She smacked her lips together. She brushed her hair and replaced her glasses. Her hand flicked her left lapel causing a stray blond hair to descend to the floor then she left the facility. She walked straight out as if she was walking out of a chemist's shop without looking back at her half drunken coffee.

The café owner thought about reminding her of her drink but before he could call to her, she was already on the street. He shook his head. That was a sure detached woman he thought.

Angie continued past the storage facilities into the ancient Saltmarket where she found and entered the High

Court of Judiciary.

The High Court was for serious cases and would be heard by one Judge and fifteen jurors. The seven men and eight women had taken their position and been sworn in some two hours before to hear the case to be made. They had heard the evidence of three witnesses. Dr Angela Lawrence was called as the final prosecution witness. The Prosecutor Advocate Mr Gregor Dunbar QC had prosecuted many of the murderers; fraudulent bankers and now, in what was becoming more numerous of offences, a case of sexual abuse was before the Judge, Lord Prosen that day.

Angela took her position in the witness box and peered over to see the smiling welcoming face of George Price. He was on trial. She took the oath.

'Dr Lawrence your age and Profession please,' began the questioning by Mr Dunbar.

'I am thirty six years of age and the Clinical Psychologist in charge of the Hazelnut Assessment centre on the Orkney island of Rousay.'

'And your qualifications?'

'I hold a Bachelor of Science degree in Psychology from Glasgow University and a doctorate in Clinical Psychology from the same University.'

'And how long have you been in charge of the Orkney centre?

'Almost seven months now. It is newly built and I am its first director.'

'Very impressive I must say, Dr Lawrence. But now I must take you back to your early years. You understand?'

'Yes, I do,' she said with a shiver to summons up her courage. Her eyes strayed to notice the press box full of itchy penned journalists. This was Court Four, the court of the Day. The minor league cases had been disposed of in the morning sessions. Their attention centred now on Angie's evidence.

'Tell the jury how long were you a child in the Firbank Children's Home at Elderslie in Renfrewshire?' asked Mr Dunbar.

'I was there for ten years. From the age of six till I was sixteen.'

'And why were you in a children's home?'

'I was to all intents orphaned.'

'And how would you describe these years in care?'

Angie's glare seemed to fix at a point between His Lordship and the Jury. It was not a significant area of the court. It was just a plain cream wall in fact but that was the tableau on which Firbank Children's Home appeared in her mind and it brought memories flooding back. She gripped the witness box tightly with her hands steadying her shaking legs.

'I experienced every possible emotion. From sheer delight to abject misery, worthlessness,' she replied.

'You mention worthlessness.'

'Yes.... I tried to kill myself...... twice.'

The jury sat up. This was clearly going to be a crucial witness but Angie did not observe their movement.

'You tried. Did you just think about it or did you attempt actual suicide?'

Angie unbuttoned the sleeve of her ivory white blouse. She pointed.

'Here, on my left arm, I still have the scar when I tried to cut an artery. It's still visible.'

'Show the jury your arm if you please,' requested Mr Dunbar.

'Objection. This is nothing to do with the charge my client is accused of,' interjected Mr John Lever QC.

'Objection over-ruled Mr Lever. I will reserve judgement if it's not pertinent, rest assured. Carry on Mr. Dunbar,' said Lord Prosen.

Angie turned to the jurors. She rolled up her blouse sleeve once more and turned her wrist over. The Jury peered at the faded scar with sympathy etched on their faces.

'And if I may ask you to show my friend,' said Mr Dunbar pointing at the Defence Advocate Mr John Leaver QC. He glowered as he strained his eyes to make the greatest impression of seeing nothing.

'What caused these moments of sheer despair, Dr Lawrence?'

'It was Gregor. He made me suffer.'

'You mean Mr Gregor Price?'

'Yes, the accused.'

'In what way?

'He'd bath me and rub me down concentrating on my private parts. That's how it began.'

'How old were you then?'

'The abuse began, as soon as I arrived at the age of six until I left. At first I thought he was only making sure I was clean, perhaps only doing what a parent might do.'

'By twelve or so, surely you were maturing?'

'I......'

'Objection. The witness refers to her time of abuse. That was surely not the thought or word that went through a child's mind.'

'Mr. Lever, I remind you that the witness is Dr Lawrence, a clinical psychologist. You should take from that information that the witness knows exactly what abuse is in all its forms. Dr Lawrence, please continue.'

'Thank you Lord Prosen. Yes, I was physically mature by thirteen. But the bathroom lock was taken off the door. It was a Health & Safety matter we were told. In case the home caught fire.'

'Told by whom?'

'By Mr Price.'

'I see,' said the prosecutor.

'He could enter whenever he wanted, he was the manager of the centre.'

'And did you ever see Mr Price as a father figure?'

'He possibly thought that was his role but when I was thirteen he started to come into my room more frequently. We all had single bedrooms. Only the younger children slept in dorms. Yes, it was not long after I was given a single room when he first raped me,' she replied. She felt she had perhaps over stressed the word rape. How the jurors might take that, flashed through her mind.

'I know this must be distressing for you. How often did this take place, the rapes?'

'Once or twice a week, sometimes at the weekend too, if he was on duty.'

'And for how long did this situation continue?

'Between the ages of thirteen and sixteen.'

'Were you able to reason with him or try to stop him?'

Angie felt her throat tighten and her lips trembled. Her voice seemed to dribble down her front.

'Take your time Dr Lawrence. There is a glass of water ....,' the Judge said pointing to the ledge a few inches below the witness box. A court usher stepped forward and handed the water to Angie.

'Thank you.' She took a sip or two and returned the glass to the usher noticing a trace of peach lipstick at the top of the glass. It distracted her for a moment before recalling the question and uttering her response.

'No, he told me I was special to him and it was our secret.'

'And was it?'

'No. I also knew he was doing this to the other girls too.'

'They told you?'

'Yes, in their own way.'

'What do you mean?'

'We'd ask each other if Mr Price had been to see them

at night and they all said he had. They also agreed that he had touched them in different ways.'

'I see. I understand you left the Home at sixteen? Where did you go?'

'I was taken in by my school guidance teacher's family. I lived with them for two years.'

'Why was that?'

'I guess they saw I was doing well at school and wanted me to continue to get my highers. The local authority were getting rid of children when they reached their sixteenth birthday anyway.'

'So in the next couple of years you studied hard, went to Glasgow University where, after your BSc you studied for a doctorate in Clinical Psychology. Is that right?'

'My Lord this is repetition of the witness's credentials, nothing more,' said the defence agent.

'Do bear with me, I know my line of questioning is appropriate,' said Mr Dunbar.

'I hope so,' said Lord Prosen.

'I was saying it was a doctorate in Clinical Psychology that you obtained?'

'Yes, that's right.'

Mr Lever threw down his pen forcefully, sat back with his arm over the back of the chair. His acting was not evidence based. His actions were dramatic, he was being auditioned by the jury. They had to love him to get his client freed.

'And Clinical Psychology, why that subject in particular?'

'I wanted to learn what feelings motivates people. That was my first degree. The clinical psychology came later as I investigated the subject more deeply.'

'On the surface it would seem like you survived this abuse and have done academically very well. Were there any social consequences or lasting effects of the years of abuse you had in your children's home?' asked Mr Dunbar.

'My doctorate thesis was on PTSD. I was suffering from this and so I studied its causes and effects.'

'For His Lordship and the Jury Dr Lawrence, PTSD?'

'Sorry, of course, Post Traumatic Stress Disorder.'

'I see and does this impact on your life today?'

Angie felt very vulnerable to this question but she was in Glasgow far from her place of work, equally far away was her husband but at the front of her mind was the oath she had taken and the solemnity of the High Court precluded any falsehood.

'Very much so. I admit I can be very demanding.'

'Can't we all be demanding? Is that not just one's personality perhaps or the age in which we live, with its normal stresses?'

'Demanding and needing love and attention is what I mean,' said Angie to pacify his questioning but still the inquisition continued.

'Could you give the court an example of that?'

Angela hesitated and looked round the court before replying. She dropped her voice.

'Well, I send gifts to myself.'

'Speak up Dr. Lawrence. If I can't hear, neither can the jury,' interjected Lord Prosen.

'I send gifts to myself,' she said confidently holding her head up. The silence of the court digested what she had said.

'Gifts?' asked Mr Dunbar.

'Yes. Flowers sometimes chocolates, wine....'

'Does your husband see this as normal?

'Yes..possibly......probably.... he thinks it's from satisfied parents and well wishers. I actually telephone Interflora and get them sent. He's an artist with his own obsessions. He's not such a people person but a very good artist. Very good indeed.'

'And is that not deceitful?' asked Mr Dunbar.

'You might think so. I can't help it. I crave attention. It's a symptom of Post Traumatic Stress Disorder.'

'And why, Dr Lawrence?'

'Because I never had any quality attention as a child. I was an object. I was deprived of affection. I was there in Firbank Children's home to be used and abused.'

Angie's voice cracked but through determination she completed what she had to say.

'Thank you Dr Lawrence I have no further questions.

'I see it's almost mid-day. The court will resume at 2 pm,' said Lord Prosen.

All stood as the court official ordered and his Lordship left for his chambers, his sandwiches and his favourite Ribena box, kept in his chamber's small fridge.

Angie sat down in the witness box took out her handkerchief and bent low where her tears gathered in a congregation of sorrow and her sobs grew louder eventually drowning out the feet of the retiring jurors.

A hand tapped her shoulder. Mr Dunbar stood before her as she lifted her head and dried her eyes.

'Well done Dr Lawrence. You have been very brave. Keep strong for this afternoon and then it will be all over. I promise you,' he said.

♦

The afternoon proceedings resumed. The press had already settled in with fresh sheets on view to record more of the sensational case. The jurors adjusted their seating to comfortable and the lady on the extreme left polished her glasses. Dr Lawrence returned to the witness box partly pleased that she had survived her morning performance but acutely aware that the questioner this time would be her adversary. Defence council's Mr John Leaver QC stood up with his charm offensive being directed at her.

'A Doctorate in Clinical Psychology, no less. Impressive. But more likely to have been achieved from a stable and loving upbringing don't you think?'

Angie was not going to fall for this suave practitioner. Her glance was away from him.

'Or because of a determination to overcome adversity,' she retorted looking towards Lord Prosen who was note taking at the time.

'I noticed you referred to my client as, Gregor in your statement this morning. Would you refer to me as John?'

'Of course not.'

'Exactly, ours is not a relationship of friendly acceptance and trust, at this stage anyway, is it?' the QC asked with a hint of mischief.

Dr Lawrence saw this question as unworthy of an answer.

'Let me put it this way. Mr Price was the adult male role provider every girl needed in his care at the children's home. Not an easy role. Not an abusive one either but a caring, loving one. You see the difference?'

'I don't deny there were not moments of gratitude but when you say loving, it was excessive and inappropriate.'

'Like a ......too tight paternal hug perhaps?

'Sir, Mr Price was a figure of power. I could not as a child stand up to him. The consequences would have been unimaginable for me, a child in care. Where else could I have gone? Where else could I have been sent? There were no other options.'

'But neither as an adult and of course, as a child at that time, you did not come forward with any complaint. Why should we believe anything happened now, after all those years?'

'Because I am mature now, able to face these questions? If you doubt my evidence Sir, let me inform you. Mr Price has a mole, the size of a drawing pin head, on the shaft of his penis. It is situated on the external spermatic fascia. How do I know that? Do you wish me to answer how often I saw it? How often I was made to handle it? And tell you what he did with it and where he placed it?'

The court room froze recognising the significance of the statement in mouth-gaping intakes of breath for all present except two individuals. Women of the Jury held both hands to their mouths to soften gasps.

Angie continued. 'Well do you wish to ask me about these horrible events seared and scarred into my mind? Do you?' asked Angie with eyes glazed and her voice strong and accusative.

'Dr Lawrence, I ask the questions not you.......I have...... no further questions, my Lord,' said Mr Leaver returning to his armed chair.

John Leaver looked up at Gregor Price. Gregor sat with his head in his hands. Leaver waited till he caught his eye. He stared at his client with raised eyebrows as if to say he had fully understood Angie's damning statement. He could no longer defend him. Damage limitation, he thought the best way forward.

'Your Lordship, may I have a short adjournment with my client?'

His Lordship looked at Mr Dunbar. No objection was coming forth.

'Very well, a fifteen minute break?' his Lordship regulated.

Angie stood down and sought Mr Dunbar's explanation of the adjournment.

'It is more than likely that Gregor Price does not wish any further evidence to be heard. He may admit his guilt to the Crown. He may feel he will get a lighter sentence this way.'

'And will he?' she asked.

'Not in the current political atmosphere of such sexual and abusive crimes against children,' he replied.

◆

At forty-five minutes after 2pm that Wednesday afternoon, Gregor Price admitted his guilt. He was sentenced to twelve years behind bars for a historical era of child abuse of the children in his care, at Firbank Children's Home, Elderslie. He would also have a life subject to supervision after release and remain on the sexual offenders books.

TEN

Angie was glad to leave Glasgow and return to Rousay late that night. It was autumn. The angry seas and mauve heather land hid from sight on her arrival but would re-appear in the morning, fighting to banish the previous day's anguished revelations.

Sam was engrossed in the seasonal summer violence of the weather. It made the seas' sharp focus enticing. He also had news for Angie on her return.

When the front door opened, Sam rushed to welcome home his wife. She received one of his warm embraces and had never felt so much in need of his attention.

'How did it go?' he asked innocently.

'Too much to tell. Not tonight darling. Tomorrow perhaps. What's been happening in my absence?'

Sam took her coat and hung it up on one of the pegs behind the front door. As he did so he turned round with a broad smile.

'I've been offered a stand at the Kirkwall and St Ola Community Centre, their Christmas Fayre.'

'That's great. Should be the best time to sell, in the weeks before Christmas,' said Angie as she kicked off her black heeled patent shoes.

'There will be a host of arts and crafts, books and teas to make browsing enjoyable in the early Christmas weeks,' said Sam who had a target and winter focus in mind. He was motivated.

But he also wanted to inquisitively questioned Angie about her court experience. He didn't want to wait till the next day. She had not been very open about it before she went to Glasgow. It left an unspoken area in their relationship. She had warned him it related to sexual abuse in a children's home. Nasty stuff. But he was curious nevertheless.

'So were you the expert witness in the case?' Sam asked, pouring a dry sherry.

'Expert? Well yes ...in a way.'

'Who was the accused?'

'Gregor Price.'

'So was he in a children's home, the Manager?'

'Yes.'

Sam offered Angie her glass and raised his.

'Cheers,' he said. Angie raised her glass a few inches but said nothing and avoided the traditional clink. Sam read her moment perfectly. He began to place the pieces together from what he knew of his wife's past.

'Not Firbank surely?'

Angie nodded without having to answer. Sam put down his glass. He took hold of her in his arms.

'Oh no, no...you were a witness as a child weren't you. Not an expert witness...is that right? You were a victim of abuse?'

Angie's tears preceded a loud cry of anguish. Sam held her tighter and caressed her suited back in a circular massaging movement.

'Oh darling, I am so sorry for you. So dreadfully sorry that this could have happened to you.'

Their clinch lingered a full three minutes as Sam accepted how it had been information hidden from him. It was so painful for her to recall such events. Honesty in marriage had its limits he concluded and he was glad to accept the hidden secret in these circumstances. Then Angie stepped back and smiled through the tears.

'Had it not happened........I would probably not have been a psychologist.'

'If only it hadn't happened. If only....'

'If only yes and no. I know what many of the children here have suffered. I feel I'm the one that can help them more than any other psychologist.'

'Yes, I'm sure you are darling. I'm sure you are.'

Sam gave her cheek a kiss.

'Would it help to talk over the day's events?'

Despite the lateness of the hour, Angie felt it might help. She moved towards the wicker settee facing the bay. It was dark but the flicker of a light, a passing ship perhaps, made her eyes water as she focussed on the distant image. Sam sat down beside her and Arthur would not miss out either. He jumped up and sat between them. As his ears were caressed, Angie relived her Firbank years for what she made clear, was to be the very last time.

One and a half hours later, Arthur jumped off the settee. He had heard enough. So had Sam. He was glad to hear an upbeat Angie come to the end of her gruelling childhood memories.

'It's all over now. Let's toast to happy days from now on,' said Angie.

'Happy days with you darling,' Sam said giving her a one armed hug. 'And I am not concerned that these events have not been shared with me before now. You have been very brave in court today. Such dreadful things need the validity of the court system to bring closure and justice and that's what has happened today. Not so.'

Angie nodded in agreement.

He just sensed that Angie was more than glad the case was truly over. A very dark cloud had passed by.

They heard the waves collapsing on the shore. And they heard the feint rhythmic crashing for a few minutes longer, before they retired for the night.

♦

'They are showing some of my work at the Tate Modern at the end of the month. Mind if I go down?'

'Of course not Sam. Why should I?'

'I got a call two days ago from the Society that they are doing Fringe artists. That's what they are calling us. Those painting seascapes, mountains, that sort of thing. Artists based around the coasts and byways none from the cities. '

'That's amazing. I mean surely many will think you are still a city Manchester painter?'

'It seems not and it's an important reminder of what I'm doing up here. You really don't mind?'

'Of course not. As long as you love me a few times before you go.'

'Conditions accepted.'

♦

'Hello, the assessment centre,' she said. 'Really? Then I'll get the director. She's in the building somewhere. You can hold on? Ah...here she is.'

'Thank you Lucy,' said Angie receiving the telephone..... 'hello?'

'London Times here. Ryan Clarke speaking. Our legal correspondent was covering Gregor Price's trial and was very impressed with your performance in the witness box.'

'I see. Well, thank you very much. Thanks for telephoning,' she said almost putting the receiver down.

'But there's much more to it than that. I'd like to interview you.'

'Good heavens why?'

'Because I think our readers would really like to hear your interesting story. A rags to riches type of tale,' he commented. 'Just what readers long for.'

'Hardly rags and certainly not riches.'

'I can confirm the riches part, you will get paid handsomely,' Ryan said.

'I was putting the court case behind me. Thought it was now all over.'

'I understand. I can empathise. But we won't be putting you through an interrogation. Anyway we have a transcript of the case.'

'Hmmm that would make it easier I suppose. I need to give it some thought,' she said.

'Over the weekend? Can I telephone you on Monday?'

'Monday. Yes, yes Monday will be fine.'

♦

That night Angie shared the call with her husband. Sam had his reservations about more publicity after hearing the facts about the case against Angie's former care home manager.

'But Sam, I mentioned I'd married an artist engaged in seascapes. That might generate interest and exposure for you too.'

'Maybe. But publicity....?'

'Publicity for the Assessment centre, don't you see?'

'You have twelve beds and they are just more than half full at present. You and the students are coping. Isn't it publicity you'd like for yourself perhaps?'

Sam regretted instantly what he had just said. There was he, asking for and being given permission to go to

London to show his work and gain publicity and now he was questioning her right to have some too.

'I'm sorry, I didn't mean that Angie.'

Angie retained her guard with a smile. She felt vulnerable. She took the high ground available to her.

'Let's go to bed Sam. But I'm not in a sleepy mood.'

Angie and Sam cuddled in bed. They were united as one when all of a sudden they heard Arthur howl.

'Listen. What's bothering him? He wouldn't howl without some good reason,' said Angie. They quickly threw on loose clothes and shoes and headed out towards the Centre. Angie could see some smoke rising from the kitchen area.

'My God, it's a fire. Phone for help.' Angie threw her mobile to him. He caught it as he ran. Then Sam stopped in his tracks and dialled.

The smoke detectors announced the crisis. Lucy and Kevin aroused all the children and got them in a group one hundred yards away from the building, at the rear. The children had rugs over their shoulders. Angie reached the building out of breath.

'All children and staff accounted for,' said Kevin. Arthur waddled along to greet Angie.

'Good boy Arthur. You did well. But Kevin, what happened? Where's the fire?'

'In the kitchen. Probably electrical.'

'Yes an electric fault I am sure,' said Lucy.

In the distance the retained firemen of Rousay could be heard approaching.

'Let's get everyone up to the higher ground,' said Kevin. 'We don't want to be in the way.'

Three firemen appeared and led their hoses down to the sea. A steady flow of water entered the kitchen and the black smoke turned to white steam. Lucy looked at her watch.

'One twenty in the morning. Where can we take the children?' she asked.

'The Police. Perhaps they can take everyone to the Community Centre, on the mainland,' said Sam.

'Can you see to that for me?' asked Angie.

'Sure,' and Sam walked towards a Battenberg police car glowing like a firefly in the night.

'Oh my God. The Parrot. He'll still be in his cage,' shouted Angie.

'No he's not,' said Lucy. 'Troy has him on his arm. Look, over there.'

'Oh..what a relief....on his arm? Outside?'

'But he saved him,' said Lucy.

'Saved him? He'll be flying away soon,' she said making her way towards Troy.

Troy was sitting down on a hillock with Harry resting on his arm. Angie approached treading slowly and carefully.

'Hello Harry. Promise you won't fly away?' asked Angie lowering herself to his gaze.

'He'll not fly away. He likes me stroking him.'

'Even so Troy. Why don't you take him up to our cottage. Take him inside. I'll be up soon.'

'Okay, I'll not run.'

'Good thinking Troy. You'll manage. Sit him on the back of one of the wooden chairs,' said Angie pleased to be giving Troy a feeling of considerable responsibility.

Before too long the retained firemen were dampening down the kitchen. The sea water ensured no source of unseen flame or heat could survive. When the dousing had been completed, Officer McCallum reported.

'The fire's source seems near the gas rings. Even if all the gas rings had been left on at full, it could not have started the fire though. Somehow it was the surface shelving near the rings which was the seat of the fire.

Puzzling. Can't get my head round that one.'

'So what are you thinking Officer?' asked Angie.

'It may be a chicken or an egg situation. A wastepaper bin was burned out. But was the fire started there or was it consumed by fire? It's certainly possible the fire may have been caused unintentionally,' said Officer McCallum. 'Then again it may not have been.'

'Presumably the place is insured?' asked Lucy.

'Of course. I'd not be able to run an establishment without insurance and have health and safety procedures in place. Our fire drills have been effective, as you well know,' Angie said as though she was addressing a Girl Guide safety course.

'Yes, but it will be a police matter. They'll have to decide how the fire started,' said Kevin.

♦

The children were conveyed to the Community Centre where they were given put-up-beds. They would be at the Community Centre for some time. All meals would be taken there but the classrooms and administrative office had been left unscathed so school on Monday would be as normal as possible at the Hazelnut Assessment Centre.

On Monday, Inspector Gillies called to see Angie. She took this squat uniformed man to her room. He placed his hat on her desk and placed his brown leather gloves inside the rim.

'The forensic team have had a look at the fire. It was certainly started deliberately,' he announced with a degree of smug satisfaction.

'I am surprised Officer. None of my clients are fire raisers and given the time of the fire, all would have been asleep in the centre,' said Angie sitting up straight with her shoulders back. She was not going to be intimidated by this official.

'Be that as it may, I'll have to take fingerprints of all your clients and maybe even swabs to check any DNA near the source.'

'I cannot let you do that officer.'

Inspector Gillies uncrossed his knees and bent forward. His bushy black eyebrows covered angry eyes.

'Dr Lawrence. If a crime has been committed, I am obliged to investigate and bring the culprit to justice. That way, you will not have the same situation re-occurring.'

'I repeat I can't let that happen. These are very delicate children. Cognitive Behavioural Therapy is what we do here and the authority figures of the Police and their procedures will act against the work I am doing.'

'I don't follow,'

'My clients come from homes where the police have been regularly in attendance; where social workers almost lived with them; figures of authority. They have reacted badly to their treatment and that's why I have them. Your procedures will set my work back. So you see I can't allow finger prints to be taken.'

'I don't wish to pull authority on you Dr Lawrence but if you are going to disrupt my work, you may face charges yourself.'

'Do not threaten me. I assure you if anyone did set fire to the kitchen it would be one of my seven clients. So there you have it. I tell you one of my seven children started the fire. Which one? Does it matter who? And I assure you I will give a stern lecture to which you could be invited, in plain clothes of course.'

'Nine you mean.'

'Seven I said,' Angie snarled.

'And two psychologists live there too?'

'Yes but you could not possibly infer a psychologist

would set fire to the kitchen and put lives of children at risk?'

'I have no evidence to rule anyone out. The cook and the teacher will also be questioned even although they were not in the building at that time. So I assure you Dr Lawrence, my inquiry will continue.'

'Then let it be noted that I regard your intrusion as unhelpful. You will not examine my clients without my presence,' Angie said as her face grew redder and she felt her heart pound like the footsteps of Gregor Price on his way to her room. She was livid.

Inspector Gillies interpreted a slight backing down in her statement. Clearly this woman was in charge and was a force to reckon with.

'I'll leave then Dr Lawrence. I will be back,' he said stressing the future sparring match.

No sooner had the police van left when the telephone rang. Still seething with rage, Angie answered it.

'Good morning. Ryan Clarke here...the Times. Have you decided?'

Angie's rage subsided ever so slightly. How could this request have escaped her mind. She was not ready or prepared to give him a definitive and measured answer... or..could she?

'Ryan,' she said taking a couple of steadying deep breaths, 'I must admit this has not been on my mind over the weekend. I've got some reservations. Can we put it off for another week?'

'Difficult. My editor has me lined up for a host of other interviews. Can I not persuade you?'

'It will be intrusive, this article,' she said.

'Not my words. It will be truthful. It's your life, your interesting life. So back off if you wish or let's go for it. Your choice.'

'Mmmm Ryan, okay ....I'll tell you all. The whole lot. The whole bloody lot. Yes, I'm up for it.'

ELEVEN

After forensic teams had left the kitchen and the insurance company approved the repairs, the kitchen was soon functioning as before. No trace of the fire could be seen nor detected. The insurance company had paid with little resistance although they retained an open mind as to how the fire started. Harry was safely in his cage in the general meeting room and as so often, the laziest dog in the world was stretched out as only Bassett hounds can. Arthur, with his head fully extended, was occupied dreaming, sniffing and farting.

♦

Tony Arnold had been out of prison for three months and to the pleasure of his after-care social worker, had not only settled well into the flat in Glasgow's east end but he had begun to work as a van driver. Despite the incarceration and restriction of the van's two doors, he travelled far and wide in a vastly changed country. It was the very antidote Tony needed to complete his re-education. That and learning how to operate a Sat Nav which gave him instant journey routes in a strange yet familiar land. In fact it was not just a local van driver's position. He had secured employment and joined the nationwide delivery group LEL Parcels UK. (Land's End to Lerwick Parcels). They were a company always willing to give served-time criminals a second chance. LEL were confident in Tony's attitude and work rate. So Tony's bailiwick was now the whole of Scotland.

♦

Sam spent four days in London. Four days away from his wife. Four days in the London Tate Gallery on the Thames river where he renewed artistic relationships. The contrast with his new life struck home time and time again as enquiries were made about his painting settings. He contemplated his life's recent changes and questioned in his mind if it had affected his marriage. Who had gained from their up-rooting from city life? He had certainly done so as his new work was attracting much interest and as long as he found avenues to show his work, it really did not matter where he lived. On the surface being the Director of the Assessment centre had given Angie considerable responsibilities. But her past was coming to light. It was a history which Angie had largely kept hidden from Sam. Indeed he felt she kept her childhood from herself as well as himself. But now that the court case was over, the tipping point had been reached. Sam now hoped for a more settled relationship with Angie based on trust and love in the Orkneys. With thoughts of missing the sea and the sea breezes in his nostrils he rang Angie, overlooking the Houses of Parliament.

'Hello darling. All well?' he said.

'Hi, yes. How's London?'

'London's busy as you can imagine. Amazing contrast.'

'How's the Tate going?'

'Banking £15K tomorrow morning. They like the seascapes here in the capital.'

'Well done. Glad you came up here?'

'Yes, in more ways than one. I love the landscape, the Island, the solitude...I just wonder if I'd be selling any city scenes in London. You know the coals to Newcastle syndrome.'

'Still another day selling?'

'Yup, let's see what that will bring. Glad to see so many school trips to the Tate.'

'School kids don't buy paintings surely?'

'Sure but they have parents and the kids talk at home. We've even given flyers out with our paintings and price tags so I'm forever hopeful. Well, see you in 24hrs,' he said.

'Before you go,'

'Yeah?'

'Done any of the crossword?' she asked.

'No, forgot to buy the paper.'

'Okay take care, love you..mmmm,' she said.

'Love you more than all the people on Waterloo Bridge?'

'Is it the rush hour?' she enquired but the line had gone dead.

♦

On Sam's arrival back he confirmed two other sellings bringing his total to £26K from The Tate sales. It was a fraction of Angie's salary but that did not matter. The important fact was that Sam was still in the hub of the artistic world even if on its outer fringes. He arrived late on Saturday evening and Sam was tired. He slept soundly aided by an open window and the salty air.

That Sabbath morn Sam slept on. Angie got up and had breakfast. Only on Sundays did Angie find time to read the newspaper. The Saturday Times had TV listings for the week but the television sat in their room, an unwelcomed guest for most of the week. The crosswords T2 and the Cryptic Grid focussed their joint minds with Sam usually speeding through the easier T2 before joining Angie in the brain teaser.

But in the centre of the Magazine supplement this weekend was a picture of Angela. She made herself a strong Lazy New York blend of ground coffee which she took from the fridge, sat outside the cottage on an old wooden milk churn and read of her life in care, her life after care, at university and now her life in charge of the Assessment Centre. After reading the article Angie returned to the cottage and hid the magazine under the settee. She had to reflect on what she had read. Perhaps she had let her shield down too low, even for her husband.

That afternoon Sam and Angie were completing the irksome Cryptic Grid.

'South of Sicily, can make you angry, 5 letters?' Angie asked.

'Malta,' said Sam with a satisfied smile. 'Is that it finished now?'

'Malta?'

'Yea. Malta GC, Cross, angry get it?'

'Oh yes. Just one left then. After Fun it's Sad then Funny. 7 letters. That's a hard one,' said Angie.

'I'll need to sleep on that one too.' Sam folded the paper and put it down. 'Where's the magazine?

'You don't usually read it.' said Angie.

'True, not all of it. But I like to see it anyway. I like to browse, flip through it. Have you got it there?' he asked.

'Mmmm I can't remember where I put it.'

'Really? Can't be far away.'

There was no way she could hide it any longer. But she didn't want a further interrogation.

'Just remembered.' She walked over to the settee, bent down and pulled out the magazine. She placed it on his lap and kissed him.

'The magazine. There you are. Arthur, walkies.'

◆

On her return with Arthur the interrogation was not forthcoming. The magazine lay on the sofa closed. It lay there for the rest of the day but when Angie announced she was retiring to bed that night, she noticed he had picked up the magazine once more.

By the time Sam got to bed, the light was switched off. His thoughts which he wanted to share would have to wait till the morning.

◆

Monday morning and the 7am alarm set off the hourly BBC news. They heard the headlines. "We are going to be talking to ....." Sam's finger shut the announcer up.

'Funeral,' said Sam.

'Wh..what are you on about?' asked Angie still a bit non compos mentis.

'Funeral, in the dictionary it falls between Fun and Funny. So it's sad. Funeral, 7 words.'

Angie smiled, turned towards Sam and placed her arm around him. He ran his fingers through her hair and glanced at the clock.

'You're ill darling,' he said.

'Ill me? Why do you think that? What do you think I've got?'

'I'm no doctor and I'm certainly no psychiatrist or psychologist. But that article. It all makes sense. I guess there's no need for the flowers and chocolates anymore,' he said.

Angie said nothing. She was relieved that he was not angry with her. He could have been. Her hand started to glide sensually over his chest.

'Darling, you are all I need to be cured,' she said.

'I don't understand it all. But I know you had a miserable childhood, through no fault of your own. And I'll always love you. You know that....'

'Of course...I....'

'You know that we've got to speak more, understand each other better?' Sam said interrupting her.

'You're right,' she replied.

'No more flowers, chocolates, no more wine?'

'Sam, I wasn't just a witness in that court. I've been a patient in that court. It is difficult to explain but it was the first time I could off-load the pain of being in care. It was therapeutic, in fact, it was front-line therapy.'

'I know,' said Sam still massaging her head. 'I know.'

Angie began to sob. Her tears fell onto Sam's chest. He moved round and placed his hand on her breast.

'I'm so lucky to have you, Sam.'

Sam did not reply. His interest was in pleasing his wife even more.

♦

At 11am Angie called the school together in the largest classroom. Everyone was there. They could see that she wore a sombre expression. The atmosphere was cold and a tension was obvious. Kevin seemed to read Angie's mind more than the others and pursed his lips and with his index finger resting against them, he stared at Lucy. Angie had everyone's attention. Even Harry cocked his head and said nothing.

'I had a telephone call this morning from Aberdeen Royal Infirmary. Mo died there last night.' Sorrowful gasps and tears filled the room as Angie stood unimpassioned.

'There are many whose lives we change. For others it's not to be. They don't make it. That's why Mo died. What will your story be?' Not a voice answered. Not a movement seen. Angie was satisfied with their response. It was good therapy in tragic circumstances.

The silence was broken. Arthur farted but this time no one sniggered. Harry sensed the atmosphere too and simply said, 'OOooo,'clinging to the spars upside down.

'Isn't that a bit harsh to say that?' whispered Lucy.

Angie hoped no child had heard her. She turned towards her and stared right through her eyes.

'Do not undermine me,' she said slowly, quietly and with deadly purpose. 'Go to my office, now,' Angie said with a dagger stare.

Lucy made her way to her office passing Kevin.

'I warned you. Easy, don't upset her,' he whispered.

Angie arrived at her office two minutes later. Lucy prepared for the long anticipated confrontation. The spring was fully coiled in both minds. Angie slammed the door close and sat at her desk before Lucy.

'Let's get this sorted Lucy. Is Psychology for you? Or are you for psychology?'

Lucy lowered her head. It was a very harsh question, a perplexing one and she decided not to answer.

'You are a student. You learn and read and absorb good practice but you learn all of this in a bubble. That's the academic constraint which demands that theory needs to be tested, verified and ratified. It seems you are not taking the opportunity to prepare for your profession.'

Lucy reflected on what Angie was telling her in a distracted way. She was right. Academia was not really her thing. Lucy was out of her academic depth but Angie did not really know the truth.

Angie folded a large piece of white paper. She drew two concentric circles in red and blue. The folds continued. She pressed them hard on her table.

Lucy looked on and wondered if this was her worry-bead scenario. A need to find a distraction to keep her thoughts on a straight line to conclude this awkward interrogation.

Then Angie lifted her creation and the paper aeroplane flew gracefully over Lucy's head. It veered to the right and would have glided to a smooth and perfect landing had it not met the window. It crash landed to the floor. Lucy wondered if she should retrieve the paper plane or was that not part of her game?

'Tell me Lucy, what have you just seen?'

'You made a paper aeroplane and it flew over my head,' she replied.

'Interesting words. ....over your head....yes... anything else? I mean, could you apply that to your work?'

Lucy wracked her brains to provide a pertinent answer.

'My work? Well, it might start a programme with a mute patient. Or open up a quiet individual. Perhaps encourage a child to make his own paper plane and see how he or she does. Encourage him,' she concluded with a slight drooping of her voice.

'All true but you've missed the main point of the exercise, haven't you?'

'And that is?' asked Lucy wishing to understand Angie's academic mind.

'Think Lucy. The professional clinical psychologist makes a paper aeroplane.'

There was a pregnant pause. Lucy ventured in a whisper, one last thought.

'It brings the psychologist down to the level of the patient?'

'Exactly. Because when you engage the patient, you make progress. Now I ask you have you ever learned that lesson in the university?'

'No, and the parrot and the dog. Is that's all part of the breaking down of us and them?' asked Lucy.

'Yes, although there is much research when it comes to mental health and the role of pets, particularly dogs.'

'So you think I should be as adventurous with the clients?'

'Lucy, there are two kinds of psychologists. The ones who practice psychology and the ones who need a psychologist. But they are not exclusive that way. The secret is to know when you need a councillor. We all need a councillor from time to time. Especially those who think they don't need one.'

Lucy digested Angie's thought-out words of wisdom.

'Very true. You practice what you preach. I mean, reading that Times article, you had a rotten upbringing. You must have needed someone to talk to.'

'As I said, Lucy, we all need counselling.'

♦

The Sikorsky S-92 helicopter prepared to land at Aberdeen's Dyce airport. Twenty two men sat facing each other as the ground came up to meet them. Safety belts were released and two weeks leave started at that precise moment for all of the men.

Last to leave the throbbing helicopter was Mark Pearson. As he did, a magazine on a vacated seat caught his attention. He picked it up. He thought he might not have time to get to a newsagent in the aerodrome before his next flight to London. Time was tight. The magazine would tide him over the two hour flight home to leafy Claygate in Surrey, to wife and two children.

Mark Pearson was a marine biologist and qualified deep-sea diver. He was much admired for his cold professional approach to health and safety under the stormy North Sea. He was both good at his work and excited by its nature. He was a man in the prime of life, with chiselled jaws and smiling cheeks. His black hair was receding gracefully and his six foot frame was appropriate for his testosterone driven profession. Yet at home, he was a gentle loving giant to his four year old son Oliver and four month old daughter, Jessica.

On the plane south, Mark sipped a whisky on the rocks as he flipped through the Times magazine. He read Robert Crampton's Beta Male and wondered if his Alpha Man could make an alternative weekly column. Caitlin Moran's column was as challenging as ever giving him insight into the idiosyncrasies of the female mind. Melanie Reid's Spinal column made him marvel at her social abilities in the face of such a restricted body. His pity for her stemmed from the contrasting good fortune his life continued to offer.

He turned to one of two leading articles as the plane crossed the border somewhere above Hadrian's Wall. The island of Rousay he thought. Not so far away from work. The island had been captured on a favourable day. A daytime shot capturing the vibrancy of the green pastoral and archaeological land, a rocky foreshore and a sunset over the rolling sea must have been bliss to the Home Counties readership. It might even cause interest in future holidays for some browsing the magazine. Mark read of the 12 bed assessment centre and its director, Dr Angela

Lawrence. He looked at the picture of her, he lingered at the picture studying her facial dynamics then read her story. He reflected on the rise from rags to riches of this academic woman six years his senior but one aspect seemed to haunt him. At first he could not quite put a finger on the irritation. But the name Angela rang a bell deep down in his mind.

TWELVE

Sam reflected on his wife's recent exposure. She had come a long way since those heady loving days in Manchester when every penny counted. Now a sky high salary which her post had brought seemed to have detached her from reality at times. That she was the Director gave her a further boost which left Sam behind within his own artistic world. Which of them was set on an even keel for the future? The question played on his mind. It was not at all clear.

The flowers and the chocolates were no longer arriving and so he gave her more attention to compensate, as best he could. He began to understand the influences behind her becoming a psychologist and wondered just what she would have been had life not thrown so many arrows at her. Inspired by these thoughts, Sam opened a new sheet of his pad and with a broad black stroke began a surreal angry picture. One which confronted daemons. Real and imagined daemons. It was a work which needed no vista. It was one he could work on in the cottage in the dead of night, in all weathers. For the time being, gone were his landscapes and seascapes. He was working well outside of his comfort zone, but enthused by his subject matter.

◆

Mark sat down in his conservatory. A robin emerged from the hydrangea nearby to announce its presence and the last of the admiral butterflies left the waning white buddleia bush. Autumn advanced but at mid-day the conservatory retained some sunny heat. He took his mobile from his shirt pocket. He scrolled through the contacts to his widowed Mother.

'Hi Mum. All well?'

'Yes darling. And you? On leave?'

'Yes, back in Claygate. I'm ringing because I have a matter on my mind. How can I put it? I'm thinking of my past.'

'Why we adopted you? That's easy,' Shirley said in a matter of fact way.

'Yes, I know that, Mum. But before you got me, what was my name, where did I live?'

'Darling that's in the distant past. You have always been part of our family.'

'Yes Mum but what was my name before I was adopted?'

'It always was Mark,' she said.

' Mark what?'

'Oh dear, I can't remember.'

'Try Mum. It's important to me,' he said.

'I've still got some of the original papers in the deed box, in the attic.'

'Can you get them for me?' asked Mark.

'I suppose so. Or you can come over, go up and see what's there.'

'Oh then just one other thing. Did I have a sister, about six years older?'

The line went silent.

'Mum, are you still there?...are you crying?'

'Why are you asking these questions, Mark?'

'Because I may have discovered my sister Mum. Wouldn't that good?'

'But that's not possible. You must be mistaken.'

'Why?'

'Your sister was placed in care. We have no idea where she will be. Maybe she was adopted or fostered, and by now happily married. I don't think you should investigate. It might bring you grief.'

'I'm sorry to distress you but it's important to me. I need to know. So, you say, she was in a care home. Was my sister's name Angela?'

Shirley removed her glasses and wiped her tears. 'That's right....... it was, it was indeed, Angela.'

'Don't worry Mum. It's going to be okay. I'll come round tomorrow.'

♦

Kevin met with Angela in her room at her request.

'Your Glasgow tutor hopes to visit next week.'

'Ah, Dr. Ewan McKay,' said Kevin.

'Yes, I gather he's your academic supervisor. So, how do you think it will go?'

'Pretty well, I imagine. He's easy to get on with, Ewan.'

'Yes?' said Angie.

'I think you are innovative. And that brings results. I think he might learn a lot by visiting here,' suggested Kevin.

'Examples?' asked Angie.

'Sal for instance. She's come out of her shell. It's Arthur and Harry that have done most of the work however. She's a real animal lover,' said Kevin.

'Then a placement at a Kirkwall vet's practice is not out of the question?' asked Angie.

'Maybe, maybe not. I'll have to prepare her for that though.'

'Of course, good.' Angie twiddled her pencil and stared out of the window.

Kevin realised Angie's agenda was stalling.

'Don't worry, I'm sure the meeting will go well. Has Lucy got a date with her supervisor yet?'

'That's proving a problem. Can you send her in?'

'Sure,' said Kevin smiling back to the smile she gave him.

Lucy arrived without any warning about the purpose of the meeting. This time Kevin's words to her were brief as he gave her the instruction to report to Angie.

'Tutor visits, that's all,' he said.

She knocked on Angie's door.

'You don't need to knock Lucy. Just enter.'

Lucy felt an atmosphere could be brewing once more. She nervously played with her hands on her lap hidden by the table.

'You are not a student are you Lucy?'

Lucy dropped her head.

'I've contacted Edinburgh University, Napier and Herriot-Watt universities. Lucy you are not enrolled in any of these. How the hell did you find yourself here?'

Only tears and sobs came from Lucy while Angela waited for an explanation. Angie was angry with herself more than Lucy for not getting an answer to this conundrum sooner.

'I was expelled from a Childhood Studies course at ....Edinburgh College. ....I was supplying drugs to students,' said Lucy eventually through tears.

'Why, for goodness sake?'

'I was depressed. There were too many expectations on me and I was failing.'

'Expectations?'

'My father is an Edinburgh surgeon and my mother is a lawyer. I was the one with no brains in the family. I didn't do well at school. I got into the wrong crowd and that's where I got into the drug scene. It happened so quickly. So very quickly.'

'But at the college?'

'I needed only a few O grades to get into the College. It's not university. I lied to you. It's an establishment for hairdressing, manicuring and childhood studies for nursery staff. It was a childhood studies course I did. I loved the psychology lectures and did well in that subject. But students wanted their highs for the weekend and I got them easily through my contacts.'

'Okay, I understand the pressures. But how on earth did you find yourself up here?'

'After I was thrown out, I was in Glasgow, living with a former school friend. I was passing the university. It began to rain hard so I went into the Bute Halls for shelter. It was there on a notice board where I saw this placement being advertised. I made enquiries about the supervised placement and they told me Kevin Mensah had already got ' t placement. They even told me his starting date, so I thought I'd come the same day and say I was from Edinburgh. That implied the university of course. I thought Orkney would break me away from the drugs scene and it has. I thought I could tag along and do something in child care, pretending to be a psychologist.'

'My god. You certainly had a brass neck,' said Angie.

The sobs kept interrupting her words. 'So you .... knew.... all along?'

'Let's just say I was suspicious. I didn't think you had it in you. But I did see some value in your work. You are good with the children. They have taken to you. That's plain to see. You are more of a people person while Kevin is the academic.'

'So, are you sending me home?'

'What good would that do?'

Her reply took away Lucy's preparation for expulsion. Had she heard correctly?

'You could be an assistant, a help to Kevin and a general dogs body around here if you want. I believe in giving second chances. Taking risks. You know that.'

Lucy's hands gripped the chair in astonishment. She leant forward with her eyes open like a night owl.

The sobs dried up. 'Really?'

'I'm taking a giant leap of faith with you Lucy. Do I make myself clear?'

'Yes, I understand. Thank you. I won't let you down. I promise. I really won't let you down.'

'I think you could benefit from being here. Use it as a stepping stone. Do you follow what I am saying?'

'I think so. A sort of care assistant?'

'Yes but first, I think you must come clean with Kevin. On you go. Tell him the truth.'

'Ok,' Lucy's mind prepared to disappoint Kevin. 'I will. But there's just one other thing you should know.'

'Ok I'm ready. Hit me with it,' said Angie

'The kitchen fire....... I know who started it. At least I heard the children talking about it.'

'And?'

'They say it was Troy who did it.'

'Troy eh?'

'Yes it was Troy they said.'

'Hearsay. I bet Troy was not present when this disclosure was made.'

'No, he wasn't,' said Lucy somewhat deflated that her revelation was not gladly welcomed and Angies response seemed even dismissive.

THIRTEEN

Shirley opened her front door and gave Mark a hug. It was an embrace acknowledging that the time had come to put her son's mind at ease.

'Come in darling. I've found something of interest for you.'

'So you've been up in the loft?'

'Amid all your school clothes and sports gear, yes. Never knew why I should have kept them. You've grown out of them anyway.'

'Perhaps I should take them to the textile bank,' suggested Mark.

'No, leave that to me. I'll get it done in time. It's an emotional thing. I can't bear to part with the things of your childhood.'

Mark sat down as his mother brought a Pampers box from behind the settee.

'My gosh. I never thought I'd see a Pampers box again,' said Mark.

'Sturdy, that's what they are. Keep files erect and in good order,' she said delving in to bring out a faded green file.

'Here, I think this is what you are looking for. Have a read and I'll get you a coffee.'

'Yes please. That's great,' said Mark opening the file.

The slightly spaniel eared file contained some official note paper and some newspaper cuttings. He carefully took out all the cuttings and laid them on the lounge coffee table.

'So this is why I was adopted. I was to all intents an orphan.'

'You were an orphan Mark. Your mother was dead and your violent father got a life sentence.'

'Yes, but I have a sister. She even gave evidence against our father in Court, when she was only six. God she was brave. But Mum, why have I never been told about having a sister?'

Shirley sighed. She stood up and gazed out of her window onto the striped lawn, drooping buddleia and bountiful apple trees.

'It was a decision we took at the time. You were a baby. We felt as your sister was in the care of the local authority, it would not be fair to her to visit her brother in a family home. There was a considerable age gap too, you know.'

'But you could have adopted both of us,' said Mark taking hold of his coffee in both hands, for a moment of painful heat.

'Yes, there were times Dad and I wondered if we had done the right thing. In retrospect, perhaps we should have but we didn't. That's all I can say now.'

'Perhaps you are right. Anyway I'm more able to cope with family traumas and surprises now, as an adult.'

'But you haven't told me how this interest in your sister came about?'

'No, it came about by chance in a helicopter,' said Mark before sharing his thoughts and interest of the article with his mother.

Mark gulped down his last mouthful and smeared the back of his hand over his lips. He made his way over to the window overlooking the manicured lawn. He knew his mother's house was probably worth millions by now in leafy Surrey and he would inherit a great deal. Then he thought about Angie's years of suffering. Only now was she reaping the rewards of a professional. But she was doing that amid the turmoils of her past being exposed. He felt a mixture of pity and respect for her, fortitude and courage too. But most of all his feeling was he may be about to have a sister at last.

Shirley took the empty cups through to the kitchen, from where she shouted through.

'So how are you going to meet her? Write, text visit?'

'I'm not sure yet. I need to think about that.'

◆

Sam had taken to painting in doors. It was partly the autumn weather which caused some discomfort outside but it was his obsession to carry on with his macabre creation.

'Not your usual landscape I see. It looks quite an angry picture to me,' said Angie.

'When the creativity is there, the path must be followed,' he said.

'That's profound.'

'Yes, you inspire me.'

'Me?'

'Yes darling. I was thinking about the battles you had in childhood, the traps set by adults and the eventual rising of the Phoenix from the ashes.'

'That's a bit dramatic, isn't it?'

'No, I don't think so. Few people suffered as much as you did. And even fewer survived without scarring.'

'Without scarring? I may not be sending myself presents anymore but I still need constant loving. That's a scar I will always have,' she said

'We all need loving, Angie.'

'Funny you should say that. That's what I felt when excusing Lucy this afternoon.'

'Lucy, what do you mean?'

'She's not a psychology student. She was expelled as a student for selling drugs.'

'What? And she's still here? Not locked up in a prison cell?' said Sam placing his brush back in a dry pot.

'Yes, she has her problems but none that we can't put right.'

'Rehabilitation in a prison would be more appropriate Angie. Are you informing the police?'

'No, I'm not. Sometimes the authorities are not best to understand. I'm keeping an eye on her. She'll be fine.'

'Drugs. What would they say on Orkney, let alone if the kids' parents knew one of your staff members sells drugs?'

'She doesn't sell them anymore. She has no access to them anyway.'

'I've got your word for it. But I can tell you Angie, one wrong step by Lucy and she's out. Mark my words. Okay, it's not my business you say but if you are not careful she could bring this whole business crashing down. It sounds like she's a very loose cannon.'

'Don't be so dramatic, Sam. It's not like you,' she said moving away from him as he picked up his brush once more.

◆

Arthur strolled around the centre with his domed head aloft. With a lord-of-the manner attitude he returned via the kitchen door where his nose moved centimetres from the ground. Troy called him over.

'Come here Arthur. Good boy.'

Arthur responded to the call.

'Come here Arthur, Good boy' said Harry from his cage. Troy laughed. Nick heard the laughter and joined them. Moments later Sal appeared. They sat between the pets.

'I heard Lucy is not a psychologist after all,' said Nick.

'I think she is, but not as good as Kevin,' said Sal.

'I don't mind what she is. I get on with her,' said Billy gazing at Harry in his cage.

'I hear there will be more coming. Usual lot I suppose,' said Sal.

'Yea just like us,' said Troy.

'Yea just like, just like, just like, us' said Harry.

FOURTEEN

Mark returned to his oil rig at the Troll Gas Field. It was late October and the green seas had turned white in an angry squabble. He had learned his diving skills in the Mediterranean Sea where the warm water seemed enclosed by its ancient history and geography. There too the tribes and peoples of olive skin plied those waters from time immemorial. Those were pleasure dives.

But with dry suits, weights and tanks he had made the North Sea his remunerable worksite, too large to have been explored at every point. Too large too, his salary and too big his responsibilities. His annual bonus almost surpassed his salary. Targets were to be met and Mark always met them. He knew he was worth his weight in gold as no one else could do his specialised work but he also knew how to be generous with his wealth.

Part of his work was to inspect the pipes and ropes underwater for unwelcomed hosts and from wear and tear. He sank beneath the waves glad to be back at work. He inspected the gas pipes and saw capepods and zoo plantation in plentiful amounts. It was a good sign. Nibbling undisturbed were saithe, haddock, whiting, mackerel and herring. They cleaned the waving tubes. He swam among the fish like a paternal safeguarder. He shone his torch as he dived further down but could find no signs of wear, tear or bites on the ropes and pipes by curious sharks. But though he worked to his usual high standard of expertise, his mind was in turmoil, anxious to a degree and definitely excited.

Back on the rig Mark logged the report of his day's work. His mug of Assam tea had only a couple of mouthfuls left when helicopter pilot Peter 'Spiv' Emmerson brought a coffee to the same desk. It was his streamlined pencil-thin moustache and inverted triangular beard that caused him to earn his nickname. It seemed appropriate that a pilot should have such exotic facial hair.

'Anything interesting happening down under, Mark?' he asked unzipping his leather jacket and sitting down beside him.

'You'd soon hear about it if I had. And you? What's on?'

'A boring day ahead. Nothing listed. I just ain't going anywhere for one whole 24 hours.'

Mark finished his tea and looked at the tea leaves, swirling around as his gaze fixed on the resultant pattern.

'Looks like you're deep in thought.'

'Spiv, can you give me a lift to Orkney?'

'Kirkwall? No problem, if you mean tomorrow.'

'Tomorrow, yes but not Kirkwall. Rousay, the island nearby.'

'I'd have to check for a flat safe landing first. So, you going fishing?' asked Spiv.

'You could say that. Can you stay with me, just in case...well...just in case it doesn't pan out well and I need a quick get away?'

'You're not getting me into hot water I hope,' said Spiv with a concerned eye.

'It's a one off visit. It will end well or be a disaster. Only time will tell.'

Spiv liked a challenge and in this case one to relish. He felt the mission would be spoiled if Mark shared any further detail.

'Then I'll say 08.00 hours, okay?'

'Can you make it 09:00 instead? I don't want to arrive too early,' said Mark.

◆

Sam was still working on his macabre painting. A black oil background was now sporting flashes of colour coming from mouths and cracks. He was satisfied that it would be a work of contemplation; a hanging, chatting focus for the pre Christmas market. But where could he show his stack of eight seascapes? Not near his present work he thought. He stood back from his painting and as he decided where the next influence would take his brush, he detected a hum growing louder. He looked out of the window and saw a yellow helicopter approach like a giant bee. He watched as it settled down on the beach nearby.

The children looked out of the window and asked if they could go down to the shore and see what was happening.

'Yes but don't go too near the helicopter, your head might be cut off. If the pilot tells you to keep back, please obey him. I'll come down with you in a moment,' said Kevin.

The blades rotated slowly before coming to a halt. Two met got out and started to come ashore as the children ran towards them.

'Hi kids,' said Mark.

'On duty?' asked Kevin.

'Not really. Have any of you been on a helicopter before?' asked Spiv.

Heads shook.

'Do any of you want to see Rousay from the sky?'

There was a chatter of excitement. 'Yea can we come up with you?' asked Troy.

'I guess you are in charge?' asked Mark.

'Right now I guess I am. Dr Lawrence is the Director but I'm sure she won't mind,' said Kevin.

'Is Dr Lawrence around?' asked Mark.

'Yes, I saw her earlier. She won't be far away,' said Kevin.

'She won't mind if I take her kids away with you?' asked Mark.

'As you say, I had better come too,' said Kevin.

'Okay, let's see ...I make it seven children two crew and you, one staff member. Let's go.'

Kevin led the children to the helicopter. They were led on board by Spiv and buckled into the seats facing each other.

Spiv put on his helmet and gave the all clear for takeoff. The children gave out a scream as the land faded beneath them. They flew over the roof of the Assessment centre.

'Is that a Bassett hound I see, asked Mark?'

'Yea, that's Arthur,' said Troy.

'That's a good name for a Bassett,' said Spiv.

'And we've got a parrot too,' said Sal. 'He's called Harry.

'Seems like you are running a zoo down there,' joked Spiv.

'It seems like it sometimes,' laughed Kevin.

The flight took them over Kirkwall and over the Churchill barriers. They saw the chapel built by Italian prisoners of war and then they flew over Scapa Flow, the burial ground of the First World War scuttled German Fleet.

'Now look there. Scarra Brae. Neolithic. That's between 2,550 and 3000 BC years old. Older than Stonehenge,' said Mark.

'Wow,' came one response as other faces looked down on the historical sight with open mouths and with imaginations ticking like over-wound watches. The children could not understand how old 3,000 BC was.

Then the helicopter picked up height and headed west towards the sea. The Old Man of Hoy stood like a large slice of cut wedding cake and Spiv took the children round its marzipan top.

'I've seen that on postcards. Now I can say I got to the top of it,' said Troy.

They spent thirty five minutes airborne and as they returned to land, ears popped as the noise of the rotating blades whished. They landed once more on the shore where Angie was standing.

The blades slowed down and one by one the children jumped down and ran towards Angie.

'We've had a ride in that helicopter,' said Elly.

'I can see that. How was it?' asked Angie.

'Fantastic. Ask Kevin.'

'I hope you don't mind. It was too good an opportunity to miss,' said Kevin.

Angie smiled. 'Kevin you are going to be a great psychologist.'

'And these are the pilots?'

'Yes,' said Kevin.

The two men approached.

'Hi I'm Peter Emmerson. They call me Spiv. I'm the pilot. I hope you didn't mind me taking the kids up for a tour.'

'No, not at all. I'm all for new experiences. I'm sure they all enjoyed it.'

'And I'm Mark Pearson. I'm a marine biologist on the Troll Rigg. We both had a day off so, well...here we are.'

'Then why not be our guests. Can you stay for lunch?'

Mark looked at Spiv. 'We'd be delighted,' said Mark.

'But first, a morning coffee? With scones?'

'Better still Dr Lawrence,' said Mark.

They made their way to the centre with Mark constantly looking at Angie as she led the way.

The children drank orange juice ignoring the currant scones, Kevin, Lucy and Angie joined Mark and Spiv at a table.

'All Mark's idea and it's turning out rather well,' said Spiv. 'To think I was apprehensive at first. Ho ho ho.'

'So it was your idea to drop in on us, Mark. Did you know it was an Assessment centre?' asked Angie.

'Yes. I certainly did. And I am very pleased to have met you today.'

'You certainly did know it was an assessment centre, you say. Why would such an establishment be of interest to a marine biologist? I just can't make a connection,' said Angie.

'I think I can. I must admit. ....er...I wonder if we could have a private meeting, Dr Lawrence. Perhaps you have an office?' asked Mark.

Angie was taken by surprise but had no reason to deny his request.

'Certainly. Bring your coffee,' replied Angie leading this tall man towards her office door.

They entered and Mark closed the door behind him. Angie's hand directed him to a high backed chair.

'I trust you will see that my intentions are well meaning.'

'I am sure they will be,' replied Angie.

'It began when I read an article about your work here on Rousay,'

'Oh yes, that article,' said Angie in a long drawn deep voice. 'Turned out a good way to advertise our existence up here in the far beyond,' she said with a smile.

'I was more interested to read of your evidence in the case of the Children's Home Manager. You certainly had a very bad start to life.'

'Yes I did but that's in the past. I'm sure it is of little interest to you,' she said with a slightly sharp tongue.

'I have no interest in causing you distress or pain, Dr Lawrence, but I should prepare you for what I am about to say.'

Mark looked into Angie's eyes, looking for some hint of a similar gene as he prepared to make his life-changing statement. Angie was suspicious. She was out of her safety zone and felt her hair on the nape of her neck standing to attention.

'Both you and I were orphans. ....You were sent to a children's home ....while I was adopted by Shirley and David Pearson. You are six years older than me. I have discovered my real name..... was Mark Arnold and you, Angela Arnold, are my sister,' Mark said awaiting a positive response from her. He was keen to stand up and embrace her as soon as she acknowledged the truth, but only if she showed signs of believing him.

The signs were there. Angie's brain was ticking over like a propeller's rotating blade. What Mark said made sense to her but begged more questions. Could they wait? She rose from her seat with indecent speed and approached Mark. Without speaking since he spoke, she drew close to him and gave him a tight hug.

'Oh God...it's true...it's true. You must be my ....my.... brother,'

Tears began to flow down her cheeks on to his shoulder as she felt his embrace hold her with a clamp like security. She gave out a high pitched scream of anguish. In the room outside the coffee drinkers looked at each other. Should they intervene? Was Angie being attacked? Murdered? What the heck was going on in there? They awaited a further cry for help, or hopefully laughter. They were very confused.

'Our mother was murdered by our father,' said Angie.

'Yes Angela. That caused our separation and I feel guilty about it.'

'But why, why feel guilty?' asked Angie.

'Because I got the better deal out of the tragedy. We should have been adopted together.'

'It wasn't to be. It's not your fault. Blame the court system or the social workers but it can never be your fault Mark. You were a baby.'

'True but I could have found you sooner. I never made an effort till I read that article. Ohhh Angie, forgive me.'

'Of course I do silly, I suppose you could not have known about my life any other way. Trying to find me would have been like a needle in a haystack. There would have been no clues till this magazine article came out.'

'Perhaps. But had I discovered the green file my mother kept sooner, I would have been obsessed with finding you somehow if I could, finding a sister, no, finding my sister.'

Angie loosened her embrace but clung on to him with her arms around his waist. 'We've got the same nose,' she said with a giggle. They laughed with ease and Mark kissed Angie on her nose. A knock on the door followed. The voice remained outside.

'More coffee?' asked Kevin.

'No,' shouted Angie. 'We'll be with you in a minute.'

Angie turned to Mark and looked him up and down.

'There's so much I want to know about you. Where do you live, are you married, do you have children.....?'

'And I want to meet your husband and get to know my sister a little better, too,' said Mark.

'Ok, let's make a start.' said Angie.

'Will you tell them the news or shall I?' asked Mark.

The door opened. The group were relieved to see two smiling wet faces re-appear.

'Well what a morning. What a day. It's the day I

found I had a brother and that brother is Mark,' said Angie pointing at him.

'Well I never,' said Spiv. 'I had no idea this man brought me here for this reason, at least as good a reason as this. This is wonderful.' Spiv approached to shake Mark's hand and then shook Angie's too, followed by a kiss.

'And I can tell you all about this fine young man. The bits he'll be reluctant to tell,' Spiv said with a loud cheerful laugh.

'I'm so pleased for you,' said Kevin. 'That's just the best news possible.'

'I am genuinely pleased for you Dr Lawrence,' said Lucy.

'Thank you all. I think cook can set two more places for lunch while I take Mark over to meet Sam.'

On their way back to the cottage, Angie learned that Mark's home could not have been further away and that she was also an aunt.

'I'm afraid they will have no cousins. We can't oblige,' said Angie with apologies written over her face.

'I see. So Sam works from the cottage?'

'Yes, sometimes. He's an artist. He's there just now.'

'Yes, I know.'

She opened the front door.

'Darling, I've got a guest. Have you a moment?'

'A guest? Give me a moment to clean up.'

Thirty seconds later, still dying his hands with a towel, Sam came through to see the couple holding hands.

'Are you not one of the pilots?' he asked.

'No, a passenger only,' replied Mark squeezing Angie's hand.

'He's a marine biologist called Mark and...Sam.... you will be surprised to learn....and this is true, cross my heart....this is...your brother-in-law.'

Time stood still. His hand-drying froze. Sam

wondered for a fleeting moment if this was a mad joke which only Angie could spring on him. Was this another attention drawing game?

'Really...that means....he's your brother?' asked Sam, throwing the towel over a chair.

'Yes, isn't this wonderful?' said Angie.

Sam looked into Mark's eyes. He could no longer deny what he was hearing. 'My, this is a bolt right out of the blue.'

'Yes, had I not read that article about your wife Sam, I'd never have traced her.'

Sam turned to the varnished barrel drinks cabinet and brought out a Chivas Regal whisky bottle.

'A bit earlier in the day than usual of course you understand. But this certainly calls for a celebration, surely? Er... you are definitely not the pilot?'

FIFTEEN

Social workers arrived the following week to take Billy, Troy and Sal for re-integration home visits. Angie felt confident that Troy and Billy would settle as they were almost sixteen and would have no schooling commitments but she had some reservations about Sal. She was soon to be proved right.

In the meantime from Roxburgh came Colin; Stranraer came Zoe; from Tranent came Hazel and from Glasgow came Brian. Nick and Elly showed them the ropes but the dynamics of the centre changed. It placed everyone on edge. Lucy however was glad of the new clients. Her role would be made clear to them. It gave her a fresh start.

♦

Sam was pleased with his painting. But this cathartic artistic experience was not his childhood. It was his interpretation of his wife's tragic childhood. He had the insight to capture in paint the trauma's of his wife's upbringing. The reunification of Angie with Mark sat at odds with his creation. It seemed there was no place for a happy ending on this canvass.

'Looks like it's almost finished,' remarked Angie as she passed by.

'Yes, practically done. But I'm thinking of another. One with a less solemn approach,' he said.

'You've really got into this genre, haven't you? I mean no seascapes for the time being. I hope you'll find a market for this type of art.'

'When the attendant spirits of creativity descend, I respond to their begging, you know that. That's why I feel a more positive one is on its way.'

'You certainly understand your work. But you don't want to get hooked on this and become known as the artist who splashed colour on a pad. Don't lose the land and seascape artist's reputation you have gained.'

'Do you like the one I've just done?' asked Sam.

'It's not a seascape,' she replied.

'No, it's not,' he said crestfallen. Had she forgotten she was the inspiration of this work? It seemed so for Sam. And gone was the moment when he could ask her if she could see her life in his creation.

♦

A tearful Sal returned to the centre two days later. Her abusive stepfather had made it clear that Sal had no part in his life and her mother had taken his cue. It left Sal vulnerable with no security. Only on Rousay could she find the anchors needed in her life. Angie was left to counsel her.

'We've got to get you settled Sal,' said Angie as Sal stroked an obliging Arthur. 'I've been making enquiries. The Kirkwall Veterinary practice is prepared to take you on.'

'Really?' asked Sal rubbing her hands together. 'Did you hear that Arthur?' she said.

'We'll go easy on this Sal. I can get you accommodation Mon-Friday in Kirkwall. You'll like it. The couple who live there have both been children's panel members. They know about children with difficulties. But I reckon you can say your difficulties are now mainly in the past. You like working with animals and want to make a career of it. What do you say?'

Sal's smile told Angie what she wanted to hear.

'You are almost a healthy weight. Mind you you've got to keep your weight up. It will be hard work at the Vets.'

'But what will happened at the weekend?' asked Sal.

'To begin with, you come back here so we see how the placement is going. And of course Arthur and Harry will be waiting for you. But that time will end and you'll be in a flat in Kirkwall on your own or with a flatmate. Are you clear about all of this?'

'Oh yes. It's just what I always wanted.'

'Best if you could put on another few ounces before you start, seriously. It will be hard work lifting animals and sweeping up after the vet. I'm not sure what a vet does, as you can see. But he will have a receptionist and there will be other vets so join in making their morning coffees. Drink some with them. Be part of the team. That way they will like you Sal. That way you might get a permanent position. You have this chance. Grab it with both hands.'

'I'm really looking forward to it,' said Sal.

Angie smiled. She was pleased for Sal. Her future seemed brighter.

◆

The skies grew dark early in November. Daylight was short. Sam was torn with the thought of his first winter storm seascapes or making further progress on his second dark surreal painting. One could be done in comfort; the other would test his metal.

'Sam, I've been speaking to Mark on the phone. He's invited me, well you too if you can, to visit for the weekend,' said Angie.

'Bit soon, isn't it?'

'If we leave it any later it will be Christmas.'

'But I've got to get organised for the Kirkwall Pre-Christmas event.'

'That's all right Sam. You'll see them again sometime. I'll fly down on Friday, lunchtime.'

'It will be dark in London by then.'

'I'm a big girl now, Sam. Yes, it will be dark. But darker and sooner up here remember?'

♦

On her return from London Angie told Sam of the family gathering that night. Meeting his wife Gail and their son Oscar and daughter Sarah. At last she had a nephew and niece and Mark had a sister. It was a built-in family and Angie relished the meeting. They had gone to see The Jersey Boys matinée and had a meal at The Ledbury in Notting Hill on Saturday evening. Never had Angie eaten in such a splendid dining room or eaten so lavishly. On Sunday Mark and Angie had a leisurely stroll over the Elmbridge Commons where they caught up once more on each other's past. They returned to a surprise barbecue in Mark's back garden to which his friends and neighbours were invited. Angie realised then why Sarah and the children had not joined them. She salivated at the sight of the spread. Guests were keen to learn about Mark's sister and her life on an Orkney island. Mark drove Angie back to Heathrow and before she headed for the departure lounge, Mark held her in a hug and kissed her. They vowed to keep in touch regularly.

'Darling, I am the happiest woman in the world. I feel I am part of a family at last. It's a truly great feeling.'

'Angie, it's just what you needed. You deserved this and perhaps it has come not too late. And it has come while you are in the prime of your life. Come here,' he said.

They gave each other another bear hug. This was a new happy Angie and her broad smile shunned the angry winter fast approaching.

SIXTEEN

December's first week Rota of assignments were prominently displayed in the LEL Parcel service corridor notice board.

'Bloody hell. Kirkwall first Saturday. No way Jose,' said Jimmy. 'I'm nae spending time away fae home at that time o' year. The wife won't have it ony aither ways.'

Tony Arnold laughed. 'I'm down for Musselburgh. Home mid-afternoon on that Saturday.'

'You still on yer own, pal?'

'Aye.' There was a wicked look in Jimmy's eye. 'I see where you're comin' from,' said Tony.

'Well?'

'Ok then let's see the itinerary.' Tony read the requirements of the day. First delivery in Perth then Inverness. Then up to Orkney. Hey...take a look at this.'

Jimmy came over to see.

'An overnight in Kirkwall all expenses paid before the long trip home. Can't be bad. I've always wanted to see Orkney,' said Tony.

'Orkney's fur relics,' said Jimmy.

'Aye that's why management thought of you first.'

'Git tae fuck man,' Jimmy said punching Tony firmly on his shoulder.

♦

Harry was quick to put the new arrivals at ease. He called out their names and made woof whistles. He mimicked the BBC 2 news anthem and whistled along to Eastenders, not forgetting the strident notes announcing the soap. Arthur was not left out by any means. He was frequently walked and Angie encouraged the responsibilities the children were undertaking in doing that task. It made their class work improve. Meanwhile Kevin held consulting sessions with each child and made copious notes of their disadvantaged and disorganised previous lifestyle before prescribing an individualised work plan for each child. That was why he stressed the importance of mealtimes, bedtimes and work times. Routine above all meant an ordered life and that was missing for most children before they came to the centre. Angie was pleased with his work and told him so, often.

Lucy found herself more of a classroom assistant helping with reading and maths. Reports were favourable now that she had found her niche but her relationship with Kevin sat on a different footing. He had felt let down considerably and fooled by her deception.

♦

It was Friday and Sam set off to the St Ola Town Hall and community Centre in Kirkwall to set up his patch in preparation for the following day. His seascapes and landscapes framed the wall area and the two introspective surreal paintings were situated in the middle. He looked at his notebook and marked with a coloured blue pen, on a yellow star, the price of each work. The sea and land scapes ranged from £800 - £1,500. The prices varied as some seascapes were only sea and cloud whereas the more expensive paintings had land, hills, cottages as well as the sea. But foremost on his mind was to lower his London prices accordingly. But he was at a loss to price his other two creations.

'What price should I put on these?' he asked a home baking stall arranger.

'The ones in the middle?'

'Yes, the two that look different.'

'Well for children's scrawls I suppose they should get a tenner?' she said polishing a silver platter.

Unperturbed Sam asked a middle aged man doing very little as he wandered in the hall until his wife had need of him. Between commands he contemplated Sam's question.

'I suppose, if you have a modern house and you lived in Chiswick and liked the picture, then possibly £25K. But up here? maybe £250?'

'You think I could sell it at that price?'

'Some have the money and an eye for an investment,' was all he said before being summoned to tack a tablecloth.

Sam compromised. He placed a £290 label on each of his experimental paintings

♦

Tony's Friday deliveries had gone to plan in Perth and he set off from Inverness in good time for his next delivery. It ensured he'd reach Thurso in the evening. It was a slow drive. There were few villages to pass but likewise few cars heading either way as the hour hand approached 10pm. He arrived in Thurso and made for the quay at nearby Scrabster for the last sailing of the night. He was excited to be on the boat but a little apprehensive about securing accommodation at Stromness on the island so late at night. The crossing was rougher than he expected. It kept him from snoozing although there was nothing to see through the port window in the café area. Fifty-five minutes later, the loudspeaker summonsed drivers to their vehicles and Tony couldn't have been more happy to hear the message. It had not been a comfortable voyage.

Stromness was hardly a welcoming site. The bars were lit up but he could not see a B&B post on his brief slow drive through the town. It was dark and misty. But tiredness was his determining factor. He slipped into a lay-by just out of the town, turned the engine off, put his blue woolly hat on his head and matching woolly gloves on his hands. He wrapped himself up in a Hunting McLean tartan blanket and depressed his driver's seat until it was almost horizontal. He had arrived on Orkney, almost the most distant part of land from the Central Belt. It was a place his mind had taken him to during his confinement. But there again so had Honolulu Madagascar and Australia, real warm islands had been his escape dreams over many a year in prison. Daylight would give him an even better impression.

On Saturday morning Tony drove straight past the expansive Scappa Flow to the main town and near the centre, found the Balfour hospital. But first he entered a sea front convenience where he shaved and washed as best he could. He delivered his medical supplies and had them signed by the administrative desk staff. He then parked his van near the key side and made for the Pomona café serving breakfast. The full morning breakfast washed down with a pot of tea was just what he required. He relished every mouthful. He had all Saturday morning to spend in the town before his 4pm sailing to the mainland once more. On the café wall he saw a poster about the Christmas Fayre. That would be a warm venue he thought. Sustained by his harbour view breakfast, he lifted his collar to his neck, donned his flat cap and set out from the café.

Christmas decorations brightened the town. Dancing lights in the street winds and decorative Christmas trees in the shops provided the atmosphere. Tony walked on and came to the St Ola Town Hall and Community Centre. It was open with a welcoming bright festive front door and a convector heater beamed down on his head as soon as he entered.

Inside was a cornucopia of cottage industries. First he set eyes on the white elephant stall. Pastry elephants and Allen keys; clamped mincers and sherry glasses. His eyes wandered. He then passed the home baking stall and purchased a small bag of flapjacks. There were four pieces inside the cellophane bag, good sized and well worth the 50p which the label confirmed.

On the end wall a bookcase held the books of local authors. Children's books stood out as their authors appeared in fancy dress to entice parents to buy. Lawrence the Lion appeared in his animal attire selling his story, Lawrence the Lion Seeks Work. Another author had a ventriloquist act with an African Parrot advertising The Parrot's Tale while yet another author sat with his Pekinese dog on his lap advertising his book Take The Lead, a story about all the dogs in his life. This stall was busy, as books were often Christmas stocking fillers. And the population knew its authors.

Tony saw the tea room ahead but just before that he saw a man sitting beneath some paintings. He approached. This was more up his street.

'These your seascapes?' asked Tony.

'Yes,' replied Sam suddenly aware of a potential customer before him.

'And the ones in the middle?'

'Yes, these too.'

'They are very interesting. I see you have one with a note of depression in it.'

'Is that so?' asked Sam.

'The convex curves give it away. The colours are stark and the lines are brittle, sharp. The other one has more concave curves. More vibrant. Telling another tale perhaps. Conceptual art you know.'

Sam smiled. 'You know your art appreciation.'

'Aye, for the last few years I've taken up art as a sort of therapy. Some of my work is a bit like yours,' said Tony.

'The seacapes?'

'No, no the surreal ones.'

'Have you painted many?'

'Yes and no, not recently,' he replied.

'I don't understand.'

'Over the years I must have produced about forty something of them. As I say, I've not done one recently. But I've been busy selling them on e-bay. Your prices, they're all wrong. I can get £750 for each one, all a bit like yours.'

'Really?'

'Yes. They are open to interpretation that kind of selling power. People see in them what they want to see. They feel they can have a piece of the artist's mind. They believe in conceptual art without knowing it. Others go by their wallpaper or spaces on their blank walls and see such paintings fit.'

'And you see depression in that first one but not so much in the other?'

'Well it's how I see it. You are the artist, what did you have in mind? But before you tell me, let me get you a tea and we can sit down for a chat. How does that sound?'

'A good idea. Yes, certainly,' said Sam who had no other customer to attend to.'

'I've got some flapjacks here to share. I've just bought them.'

'Great. Make mine a coffee, black no sugar thanks,' said Sam wondering how to respond to his thought provoking question of a few minutes ago.

Tony returned with a tray bearing a pot of tea, a jug of milk and a coffee. He lay the tray down on the table as Sam found an extra chair.

'There we are. Bye the way I'm Tony. You won't have seen me around in Kirkwall, I'm a courier van driver with LEL. Furtherest north I've been in my life. And you?'

'Sam Lawrence. I'm an artist on Rousay.'

'That another island?'

'Next nearest in fact. LEL. What does that stand for?'

'Lands End to Lerwick.'

'So you cover the whole of the UK?'

'Yes and no.' Tony laughed loudly. 'You must think I'm always coming away with yes and no answers but as a van driver, I have Scotland only. That's big enough for me. Mind you I might get the occasional Northumberland or Cumbria delivery as well.'

'So if you are on the road so much, how do you find time to paint?'

'To be honest, I've not painted for a few weeks now. Not since I started this new job.'

'I see. You were asking about my inspiration for these pictures?'

'Yes, that interests me.'

'Well, my wife was a child in care many years ago. They did not treat her well. I can leave that to your imagination. She had a very difficult upbringing. Years of psychological, physical and emotional torture. That's the first picture.'

'Yea, I get that. Have a flapjack.'

Sam munched his gritty cake then washed it down with a mouthful of coffee. He was gratified that the painting made sense to someone.

'Then her life changed about. She got promotion, found her lost brother, got rid of her daemons and has turned into a much more balanced woman. Hence the second painting.'

'Yup I get them. I guess you're talking about £800 each perhaps?'

'On E-bay?'

'Not yet. See how the market trends. Paintings have a longer sell by date than books. Don't rush it. Probably too late for this Christmas.'

'You impress me with your knowledge of painting. Where did you train?' asked Sam.

'I had some talent as an artist at school. If they put on a play, I'd paint the backgrounds too. Never thought of it as a career. It was thought to be a sissy thing in those days. I got teased about it. I put my brushes away and gave in. Pity I did. Cos I soon ended up in trouble. I actually joined a gang.'

'Was this in Glasgow?'

'No, no. Nearby, Kilmarnock in Ayrshire,' Tony said.

Sam felt queasiness come over him. Kilmarnock. Gangs. Tony..Tony what?

'Ok so you got into trouble?' investigated Sam.

'More ways than one. Drink was one problem and attitude another. I know hard to believe isn't it?'

'Well, we all mature. So it sounds like you did time?'

Tony drank his tea slowly. He replaced his cup on his saucer with extra care.

'I did time all right. Twenty six years of it. Twenty six years of regret. Twenty six years to get it right when I came out.'

'And it's coming together now?' asked Sam.

'I've got a job I like and a house. I don't drink. I've been weaned off that years ago. It was when I was inside I started art again. Therapeutic, they thought it might help. I don't think they knew how therapeutic it would be for me. It gave me a new personality. I'm grateful for that.'

'When did you get out?' asked Sam.

'A couple of months ago. Early days. But travel and meeting normal people makes me appreciate them, makes me feel part of life again. I feel alive now, at last.'

'Tell me, twenty six years is a long time. It must have been something serious.'

'Well, if you really do want to know. It really pains me now. To think I murdered the woman I loved.'

His words clicked. Sam was now convinced he was actually sitting beside Angie's Kilmarnock father. Sitting beside his father-in-law, sitting beside an artist and a reformed murderer. He delved slightly more deeply into Tony's life.

'And did you have any children?'

'Aye one beautiful daughter. God knows where she is now. Married, a mother, something and somewhere like that. I last saw her as a kid of five or six. And I think maybe a wee boy, but... I never knew him.... maybe he wasn't mine anyway. '

He pushed the tray forward and began to stand up. 'Anyway, enough of this. I'm taking up too much time for you to sell your paintings. I'd better go to the loo now,' he said.

'Can you leave me a forwarding address?'

'Sure. Just hang on a bit. I've really got to go after that tea.'

SAM ~~Tony~~ wondered if he should ring Angie and give her this news. No, he needed to speak to her and see her reaction, be prepared for her disbelief and perhaps anger. He could not gauge her reaction from afar. And he had to decide what to say. These thoughts would distil in his mind and formalise as he drove home that night.

Tony returned a happier man.

'That was quick,' said Sam

'Waterworks plays tricks these days. The urge to pee is often not very productive, lots of false alarms,' he said with an explanatory wink in his eye. 'Now you want to exchange addresses?'

'Yea, that would be cool.'

Tony wrote his home address and mobile number on the back of his LEL business card. He handed it to Sam.

'Glad to hear from you anytime. Special rates for packages too. You can safely post your paintings through us. Just get in touch when you're ready,' he said.

Sam read the card. 'Thank you Mr Arnold. I'll certainly bear you in mind. It was a pleasure meeting you. I'm sure our paths will cross again, before too long.'

'Yes, I hope so too. I've enjoyed a good chat. Take care,' Tony said turning away as he did.

A few minutes later, arriving almost too soon to have disengaged from his first encounter, a man in a tweed jacket and checked shirt asked to have a word with Sam.

'My name is Oliver McIntyre. I live in London but I'm an Orcadian. You live locally? And you did these paintings?'

'Yes, I live on Rousay and that's my artwork.'

'I like your paintings. Your seascapes. They speak to me. I wonder, can I commission you to paint The Old Man of Hoy?'

'Commission me?' These were words Sam had not heard for some considerable time.

'Yes. A frame about 36 inches by 33 inches in oil? If you can do it by next May, then I'll give you £38K and some company shares. Interested?'

'My word. Blimmey. That's serious business, you're offering.'

'You are a professional artist aren't you?'

'Hmmm yes, of course. I can do that. Any specific

angle of the Old Man?' asked Sam as he noted the dimensions and held back his excitement.

'Just as long as he's recognised as The Old Man of Hoy. Here's my card. Oh and can I purchase that seascape on the left?'

'This one,' pointed Sam.

'The very one. You take a cheque?'

When Oliver McIntyre left the hall with his seascape painting under his arm, Sam punched the air with both hands. Bingo was the word that came to his mind.

SEVENTEEN

Sam arrived back at the cottage at 6.30pm that night. Angie was in the kitchen boiling broccoli and carrots to accompany the roast chicken. She sipped a glass of Merlot as she oversaw the final meal preparations.

'Can you carve?' she enquired.

'In a minute. I'm in the loo.'

After the flush and hand wash Sam came to the kitchen and looked for the carving knife.

'Well was it a success?' she asked.

'I got a commission to paint the Old Man of Hoy.'

'Well, that sounds good.'

'£38K,' he said. 'And if I complete it by May I get some shares in his company too. Fantastic eh?'

'His company? Wow. That's brilliant darling. And the company is?'

'He's an exiled Orcadian. He's a consulting actuary with Martin & Ablewaite in London.'

'Well, have you hit the bull's eye?' she said pouring him a glass.

'And he bought one of my seascapes too.'

'You're kidding. You are certainly in the money. Bet that was the highlight of the day.'

'No, it wasn't. Far from it,' said Sam but it was not the moment to shock Angie.

'Hard to believe. Really?' she said clapping her oven-gloved hands together.

'Let's get the chicken on the table first,' said Sam.

Angie lifted her glass and positioned it for a toast.

'To this successful day. With many more to come,' she said.

'I'll drink to that. Cheers,' said Sam.

'So there's more?' said Angie serving the carrots then, with a sauce spoon, her garlic-tomato mixture.

'Yes I met a man. An interesting man. An artist....'

'Good, you have been out of their community for too long.'

'Maybe. He saw in my avante guarde pieces things I had not fully realised. He was a good art critic. Thought I had a good conceptual eye.'

'That's encouraging. Live locally?'

'No he lives in Glasgow. He's with a delivery group. He brought his van up to the Balfour hospital with some deliveries. He had an hour or two to spare so he came to the Christmas Fayre.'

'Had you heard of him?'

'Yes and No...' Sam laughed. 'That was one of his sayings actually. Yes and No. He paints these deep psychological canvasses and sells them on E-bay. Gets a good price too apparently.'

'So is he a real artist on hard times running a van or selling his paintings on his tours?'

'I tell you an interesting man. A man content with life.'

Sam hesitated. He placed his hand in his shirt pocket. His fingers poked around to secure the card.

'Be prepared for a shock Angie. A real mind-blowing scare to blow you over. Be warned. You ready?'

'You're teasing me' she laughed.

'No Angie, I couldn't be more serious, honestly.'

Angie put her wine down on the round cornflower

coaster. The atmosphere was taught, charged with instant silence yet she had no idea what to expect. Sam handed Tony's LEL business card. Her response was quick.

'Tony ....Arnold....Tony Arnold...artist?' she looked at Sam with penetrating eyes. 'Bloody hell. You met my father? He's an artist? I can't believe this happened in Kirkwall.'

Sam nodded and awaited a deluge of questions.

'Is he still on the island?'

'No his van got the afternoon sailing to the mainland.'

'My God. He's served his time.' She turned on Sam, 'Did you mention me?'

'No no no. The time was not right. But I tell you Angie he was not the man you remembered as a child. Time has made him think. He turned to art in prison to see his years through. Now he's found work and he's getting his life together.'

Angie could not eat anymore. She had to consider what she had heard. 'Arthur...Arthur, come here. Let's go for a walk.'

'Can I come with you?' asked Sam.

'No Sam. I need to be alone. You stay and eat up. When you're finished, clear up for me, yea?'

'What about your dinner?'

'Later ....later.'

◆

Next day, Sunday morning, the alarm was set for 9am. But Angie had been awake since six. Her mind was still in turmoil. Snowflakes began to hush outside, giving a brighter glow through the bedroom window. She waited till Sam stirred. He turned over and realised she was sitting up, dressed in bed.

'You said he was civil?' asked Angie.

Sam took a moment to think what she was talking about. He turned over on his back. The previous day came back to him as the urge to get to the bathroom roused him from bed. As he entered the ensuite his thoughts had returned in an orderly fashion.

'Darling, I only spent forty minutes with him, over a cup of coffee.'

'And not a word about me?'

'Honestly, I said no. I meant it.'

'Had I been with you yesterday and he discovered us, how do you think he would have reacted?' she asked.

'That's not fair, how can I answer that? You're the psychologist, not me,' said Sam.

'Just try to imagine.'

Sam pulled the plug. As the hot tap hit his soapy hands he shouted through to his wife.

'Well, he'd be overcome. Shocked. But if he realised who you were, I can't see him standing off from you. He'd either collapse in tears with guilt or throw his arms open to you.'

'No he wouldn't. He'd wait to see how I'd react first.'

'And how would you have reacted?' he asked.

'I just don't know,' said Angie.

EIGHTEEN

Angie entered the centre a little after 9am. She had hardly time to take her coat off. She had interrupted something. What it was, she could not be sure.

'Please take a seat. You will be seen in a moment,' said Zoe, with a pointed finger at a chair. Angie did as she was told.

'Next please,' demanded Colin, a frail smiling boy. Kevin brought his chair forward, turned it round and sat facing Hazel. She sat close to Kevin and blew into his eyes.

'Got it, you're at the optician,' shouted Brian and the game was over.

'Ok break over. Back to class,' said Kevin. The pupils set off giggling and talking about the charades they had played.

'Good start to the day, Kevin. Get them thinking outside the box and you've made a breakthrough. Got a moment?'

'Sure.'

They retired to Angie's office.

'How many will be staying for Christmas? She asked.

'I can't see any wanting to go home except Hazel.'

'Can she make it?'

'In a way Christmas has come too early for her.'

'Yes, I'd prefer to keep her here for at least three months. Kevin, ring her home and tease out their expectation. Try and dissuade them. Ok?'

'Right.' Kevin looked at Angie with concern.

'You are not yourself today, are you?' he asked.

Angie looked up at Kevin. She shook her head and tears began to fall. Kevin was taken aback. He stood up and stood behind her. His large hands caressed her shoulders for a few moments before Angie stood up and rested her face against his chest. Kevin's all embracing arms enfolded Angie. It was a hug of support.

'I've found out where my father is,' she said. 'I last saw him in the dock in court some twenty six years ago. I've to decide what to do next.'

Kevin gave Angie a pat on the back then released himself.

'Oh my God. So soon after meeting Mark. Wow. Angie, life is throwing its problems at you. Let me think..... at one level it's an easy decision. You have to decide to see him or not. You take it from there.'

Angie saw Kevin on the other side of her desk leaning forward with his arms extended leaning on the surface.

'Let's get out of here. Let's get some fresh air.'

They donned their heavy winter attire and Kevin's gold and black university scarf rounded his throat twice. They set out towards the sea. The clouds silently raced by overhead. Two puffins streaked past them. Flecks of white water darted into view then disappeared as the tide flowed. The grass was winter short but all bent landward. Cottage chimneys pouted out white peat smoke. The only contrasting colour was the slow progress of the red royal mail van as it headed towards the other side of the island. A large boulder gave them partial cover from the eye watering wind. They sat down close to each other.

'I've made my mind up. If I don't confront him now, he will always be on my mind. I want to keep a track on him, now that he's out of prison.'

'Ok, I've got the picture. But keep it on your terms. Don't meet at his place.'

'I do not want him here in Rousay.'

'No, I don't mean that. A neutral place near where he lives,' said Kevin.

'In Glasgow?'

'If that's where he lives. And I don't think you should do it alone. Take Sam with you.'

'Sam knows him. It was Sam who found him.' Angie smiled seeing the path ahead more clearly. She rubbed Kevin's tightly curled hair. 'You know, I think that's why you are so clever,' she teased.

'What do you mean?' asked Kevin.

'Your curls. It means your brains can't escape.'

They laughed. They knew the value of talking and listening. The bread and butter of their work.

♦

That night after they had eaten and washed up, they retired to their sitting room. Sam brought a glass of water to Angie.

'Ready? Shall I dial?'

Angie nodded and took a deep sigh then a sip from her glass. Sam read from Tony's card and dialled his mobile phone. Angie moved nearer to hear her father's voice after all these years. Would she remember it? The phone took a few moments to answer.

'Hello?' the voice said giving nothing away.

'Hi. Sam here, up on Rousay, Orkney.'

'Oh yea. Hi Sam. How's it going?'

'Fine. You well?'

'Yea, getting sorted out as you know.'

'Good. Yea we're fine up here,' reiterated Sam.

'So it will be about painting eh? You coming to Glasgow?'

'No, no plans for that in winter, perhaps in the spring. But it's not really about art I want to talk about. It's about my wife,' began Sam.

'Your wife? Is she all right?'

'Yes, yea she's fine, well perhaps not so fine, a little confused perhaps. Did I tell you she runs a centre here on the island?'

'Aye that's right. A clinical psychologist, brainy woman, I think you told me,' said Tony.

'Yea, that's Angie and I have been married for eight years now,' said Sam getting a finger stabbed in his back. 'I mean nine years. How the years fly by,' he said laughing to cover his mistake.

'Aye for some, but nine years isn't that long you know?' Tony replied recalling his incarcerated years.

'Yes we've been Mr Sam and Dr Angela Lawrence over these years. But of course that was not her maiden name.'

Sam paused but Tony's silence meant he was still none the wiser.

'Ok sure,' said Tony.

'It will come clear I assure you Tony. Dr Angela Lawrence was married and given away by her Guidance teacher, because her father was in prison. Tony, I married your daughter, Angie Arnold.'

The line seemed to go dead. Angie strained to hear his response. Sam handed the phone over to Angie and he sat behind her caressing the tension packed in her shoulders.

She heard him cry. Her training left her in little doubt that these were not crocodile tears. Her father was in emotional pain.

'Dad,' she said.

After a few more moments as Tony digested his daughter's voice, he replied.

'Angela?'

'You ok?'

'I'm sorry, truly sorry.... the pain I've caused. It's all my fault. Believe me, I am sorry and I don't deserve your pity.'

'You know, if I had grown up without the incident, what would I be? A shop keeper? A mother on benefit with three kids? I don't know. But I'm not. I've tried to understand you over the years. That's why I trained to be a psychologist. It's all been about reaching this moment in time. It's not easy, not easy for either of us.'

'Angie, you are the only person left in my life. But I know I don't deserve you. I can only offer two things. The first and most important is that you're my daughter and second, believe me, I've changed, changed from that angry man, so many years ago, a lifetime away.'

'I'm pleased to hear that, I really am. But I'm not the only one, there's Mark down in Surrey. I'll have to tell him too.'

'No, don't do that Angie, don't tell ....Mark.... yet.'

'Why ever not? You are his father too.'

'Can we meet? You deserve to know the truth,' said Tony.

Angie thought for a moment. What could her father be thinking of? The phone call was not going to solve all the questions she could muster. 'Yes, then alright. When?'

'As soon as you can. Before you tell Mark,' said Tony.

'I don't understand, why can't you tell me more now?'

'I may be selfish but I really need to be able to see you to explain everything.'

Angie reflected on what she had heard, feeling it was a riddle from a delinquent child. 'Ok let me get back to you. I guess it will be a weekend you'll be free. Unless you have to drop something off on Orkney again.'

'Yes, any weekend. Angie, I mean it, I really am sorry

for killing your mother.'

At last he had said what he had done. Angie needed that admission. The cards had been played in this first round. 'Tony, I believe you. I'll be in touch.'

Angie put the receiver back on its cradle. She turned to Sam who was smiling.

'I told you. He's a nice bloke.'

'Early days,' said Angie. 'Early days.'

NINETEEN

On the first Saturday of the New Year, Sam and Angie flew to Glasgow. It was the first flight of the day. It gave them time to register at the Glasgow Thistle hotel for the weekend. Then they returned to the Glasgow Grand Central hotel in the forecourt of Central Station. Angie had chosen this central venue because of its spacious talking areas where they could converse without being disturbed. The clock approached 11am. Two minutes before the hand struck, Tony dressed in a dark brown suit, a blue shirt and a busy yellow tie looked around the foyer.

'That's Tony,' said Sam in a whisper. He looked at his wife. Angie stood up as slowly as a rising Clydeside crane. But Tony made straight to the Gents.

During his absence, Angie reflected on the glimpse of the man who had altered her life. He looked slimmer than she had remembered him. Perhaps the consequence of a strict and mundane diet in prison. Not as peely wally as he might have been perhaps but he had been out for at least a few weeks. The waiting played on her nerves. Her tummy rumbled.

'Over here Tony,' said Sam flicking his fingers at a waitress as he did. They both arrived at the same time.

'Right Tony. It's tea you take isn't it?'

Tony nodded nervously. His opening remarks had been put on hold with Sam's drinks orders.

'That's a black coffee, a latte and a pot of tea. A plate of biscuits too please,' asked a confident Sam getting the formalities underway.

'Certainly,' said the waitress bringing another chair closer to the gathering.

Angie stood up and approached her father. She took a step towards him and he did too. Angie placed her two hands on his shoulders and as she did, Tony hugged her dropping his head to be next to hers. He closed his eyes and kissed her hair.

'You're a handsome man Tony. I can see what Mum would have seen in you.'

Opening his eyes and separating, he gently ran his tongue along his lips.

'Angie, it may surprise you. I loved your mother very much. Perhaps too much. Hard to believe isn't it?'

'Don't rush Dad, ok? There will be time for each of us to get to know each other and ask the questions we each must have stored over the years.'

'Believe me this is the happiest day in my life, by far,' he said with a soft smile and deep penetrating eyes, like those of Angie.

The waitress returned promptly. A tray was placed on the table between them.

'Let me be mother...I mean I'll serve,' said Sam flustered by his saying. The ritual ensued with Tony's shaking hand offering the plate of biscuits. The cups kept their hands occupied while Tony continued.

'I can't tell you how proud I am to say I am here with my daughter. I know I had little influence in your growing years, but....'

'You had the greatest impact on my growing years,' Angie interrupted.

'Yes, silly of me. That's so very true. But I am very sorry it happened in the way it did.'

'I don't bear many grudges Dad. I just need an explanation,' said Angie holding her head at a slight angle of encouragement.

'Am I right to think you want to know what happened that night, all these years ago, or not. I don't want to upset you?'

Angie smiled.

'I'm a clinical psychologist. There's nothing that shocks me, even if this will be so very personal.'

'Then I remind you again that I loved Margaret. But I found out she was seeing another man. I could not bear to think I might lose her. Then she told me she was pregnant. My world collapsed. There was much doubt in my mind and I guess hers too. Neither of us was sure who the child's father was.'

'So that's why you did not want me to tell Mark?'

Tony nodded firmly. 'Why put him in doubt? Why bring misery into his life?'

'But Tony, even so, he is my brother or half-brother.'

'Yes and it may be he's my son too but I always had my doubts. Even as a baby there was something different about him. Whether it was in his eyes or his hair colouring, something told me he was not mine.'

'Even so, don't you see? You say you only have me but no matter what you think, you also have a son or step-son, in Mark, cos he had to have a father.' said Angie. 'That's why he was adopted.'

'At the time I could not accept this new child. I suspect Margaret knew who the father was but never said. Perhaps had she said the baby was not mine, perhaps we would have split there and then. Had she convinced me that the baby was ours and she'd not see this guy again, then we'd perhaps still be together.'

'So that's why you killed her?'

'Angie, I hit her head. I didn't mean to kill her. I should not have hit her at all, I know, but it was only one blow to the head. If there's one thing I can say without fear of contradiction is that it's far too easy to commit murder. That was never my intention. It was my jealous spiteful hatred that surged through my fist that night. But it was, only one fatal blow.'

'I don't want to hear any more about the murder,' said Angie.

'I respect what you are saying but you need to know it was not a torrent of blows that killed your mother.'

The moment lay silent for all to digest. Then the station loud speaker announced the arrival of the Birmingham train followed by a general reminder not to leave baggage unattended and to report any suspicious package to the police.

'Let me just add a few more facts. It would be easy to say I've served my sentence, it's a new page and all that. But in fact it's true. And I don't have a temper any more. I'm not a bitter man. I put my time inside to good use to make me a better man. That may not make me a better father than before..... that's too late anyway. Perhaps I'm not needed...but if I am, then let me repeat, I am a different man. And I am still your father'

'At fifty two? You are still young. And you'll always be my father.'

'Young? Maybe.'

'So what do you want to get out of life now?'

'I enjoy my freedom as only an escaped bird can. That's why I enjoy the van job. It takes me to new places with this Sat Nav thing. It gives me a tremendous sense of freedom. Can you imagine what that feels like to me after all those pent up years? It's the best possible job getting to know the country and its people once more.'

'Perhaps,' said Angie feeling the relief she experienced when she left care. Sam nodded taking in the conversation, biting his bottom lip.

'Yes freedom with a chance, an opportunity to find family again. I had no idea it would turn out so easy. I've a lot to thank Sam for his patience that day. I'll not be coming up to stay with you of course but keep in touch, know what each other is doing. It's a human need and one I know I don't deserve.'

'Tony, that's not true. I have come to terms with Mum's death many years ago. You have served your sentence and it was long. Too long. But I get the feeling it was not a soul destructive time. I think you have changed. You've certainly matured. Whether through guilt, through art or realisation you were aging your life away in institutionalisation. But you saw that coming and you avoided it. You made good use of your time in prison. Dad, I feel comfortable with you.'

'Beautiful words Angie,' a softly smiling Tony remarked running his hand over his head through his disappeared black hair.

'I am still amazed how art and your delivery to Orkney brought you, father and daughter together. Serendipity or co-incidence I don't know but I reckon it was a good thing anyway,' said Sam.

'I can't disagree about that but I don't know how to put all this to Mark,' said Angie swirling the coffee segments around before her final gulp.

'Leave it for another day Angie,' said Tony.

'Of course I will. But it's something I'll have to clarify, and soon.'

Tony moved around uncomfortably in his seat. His discomfort was noticed by Angie but before she could ascertain the cause of his irritability, the cause became clear.

'Excuse me, I must go to the loo again.'

TWENTY

It was a few minutes after 8am. On the beach Angie strolled with Sam hand in hand. A sea breeze wafted her hair around while in their nostrils the salty air hit the back of their throats. Sam picked up a stick and threw it towards the sea.

'I'm not a dog,' said Angie.

'I know. Just getting some exercise. I don't get enough.'

'No I suppose most artists don't. But perhaps you could relax more. Get away from art for a while.'

Angie was a quick thinker. Always seeing the solution a split second before others. Impatient in a way but she would never agree to that. It was a driving energy Sam lacked and he resented being toyed around by her declarations. He loosened his hand from hers.

'You don't understand Angie. Art is not a job. It's an urge. It's something I have to do. I can't compartmentalise my work to a time-scale.'

Angie stopped walking and looked out over the water. The ripples spoke to her. 'Oh God, it's medical inspection day. I'd better be on hand.' She took her mobile from her pocket and accidently dropped it. She picked it up and shook it dry of sand.

'Hello, Kevin? Hi. It's medical inspection day today at 10 am. Tell the kids to get into their gym kits for 9.50 am when Dr. Archie Sutherland comes. Got it?' she confirmed with relief.

'Yup. I'll get them ready.'

♦

Dr Sutherland was a man in his late sixties. He had been a paediatrician in Glasgow until he retired to his native Orkney two years ago and found himself on locum duties on the islands. It was his first visit to The Hazelwood Assessment centre. He was slightly apprehensive. It was after all a residential unit for troubled children.

His Bentley parked silently in the small car park beside the centre causing a stir of excitement. A female nurse emerged from the passenger seat carrying a Gladstone bag which must have seen many bedsides over the years. She ran round to Dr Sutherland's side to take his small brief case. Now she was balanced and the good doctor had his arms to swing freely as he approached the front door.

Dr Sutherland was in tweeds, a checked brown and gold cotton shirt and a knitted brown tie. He was predominately bald with side of head grey patches. His spectacles hung on a chain dangling on his chest.

Nurse Mary McCallum was obese. No other word could describe her size. A head of red hair sat under a blue headpiece with a peal-ended hat pin securing fixture from the Orkney winds. Peely wally fair skin and freckled arms would come into view when she removed her overcoat. They stood outside the centre having rung the bell. Kevin answered.

'Oh' said Dr Sutherland surprised to see a black man opening the door.

'Come in. We were expecting you. You can use the Director's office for your examinations,' said Kevin showing the way.

'It's a much quieter place than I imagined.'

'I suspect the children are getting ready,' Kevin said hoping that they would start to appear very soon.'

'Ready?' asked the doctor.

'Yes, they will be in their gym kits. We thought that might be appreciated.'

Dr Sutherland nodded over his glasses at Nurse McCallum. 'Then send the first one in please.'

Colin appeared four minutes later still in his school clothes. Angie was informed.

♦

Angie was pleased with Dr Sutherland's medical reports. He brought to their notice that more time flossing teeth would benefit the children and that identified a supervised task for Lucy. Their cleanliness was commented on with favour and their distinctive urban accents and diction had not caused the doctor any difficulty. His years in the West of Scotland saw to that. He made recommendations for eye tests for Zoe and Brian. He also took away some blood samples and urine bottles for the lab to check but no worries were thought likely to emanate from that. The Bentley majestically rolled back up the drive with Nurse McCallum at ease in the comfortable limousine looking out to the sea. The sea was calmer now but Angie was brewing a storm.

The Centre's bell was rung instructing the children to appear in the main room. One by one they sauntered in but when they saw the anguished expression on Angie's face, they adopted a more accommodating and quieter response.

'Line up before me,' was Angie's order. 'I give you all four minutes to return to this spot in your swimming costumes. Last one down loses two minutes earlier to bed this evening. Go.'

The children bumped into each other as they set off to prepare for a swim.

'You are not taking them down to the beach in this weather are you?' asked Kevin mystified by her instruction.

Angie looked at Kevin. 'Just watch and learn.'

The children started to reappear in their swim wear. Last down was Troy.

'Two minutes fewer for you Troy. Now, I want you all to go up and dress in your school clothes with your right sock off but both shoes on. Go.'

Kevin was beginning to get behind Angie's way of thinking on this bizarre lesson but it was too premature for him to speak. He kept well out of the way when they returned and stood before Angie once again.

'Troy, do you have an aversion to promptness or do you like going to bed early?' Two questions in one sentence flummoxed Troy. Before he could reply a further command was on Angie's lips.

'I want you all back here in your waterproofs but wearing only one right Wellington boot. Four minutes, Go.'

It was a game which the children seemed to enjoy and they wondered what combination might follow their return. Troy made a determined effort this time.

'So Zoe loses two bedtime minutes this time and dear Troy I'm afraid you lose another two again.'

'But I was not last,' he said with eyes as round and wide as a grey seal.

'Troy. Look down and then along the line. Do you see anything out of place?'

The children saw the problem instantly and giggled but Troy was slow to realise the issue.

Angie raised her right hand. 'Is this my right or left hand?'

'It's your right hand,' said Colin. Angie raised her left leg. 'And Troy is this my left of right leg?'

'It's your left leg.'

'Exactly. So which Wellington boot have you on?'

'The wrong one,' Troy admitted.

'Right game over. At this rate Troy will not be seeing much daylight if we continue. All sit down. Well, did you enjoy that game? What about you Colin?'

'Yes, but I'm glad it has ended. I was getting a bit tired out and it was boring after a while.'

'And what about you Hazel?'

'It was good fun,' she said.

'So you all thought it was a good game?'

In a chorus of youthful voices they said it was fun.

'Well it wasn't meant as fun at all. You all let me down badly this morning. When Dr Sutherland arrived I expected you would have all been ready in your gym kit as you had been told. Very few of you indeed did as you were told and most of you were late in attendance. It gave a very poor account of each of you. Would you arrive at a job interview for 10:15 one morning dressed in your pyjamas and ten minutes late? I doubt it...well... after what I saw today maybe one or two of you would. So what's the message I'm trying to get across, Zoe?'

'Be on time,' said Zoe.

'Yes but that's only part of it. What's the rest? Yes, Colin?'

'Be on time and be dressed correctly and smartly.'

'Exactly Colin. This is not a game of daft fun. It's a sharp learning curve. It shows me you can dress as asked and can attend on time when you want to. Never again will you keep someone waiting and be inappropriately dressed. It's a lesson for life. One to remember. I don't want to hear of a similar attitude when Dr Sutherland returns in six months time. Is that clear?'

A chorus of 'Yes' came from solemn voices. The penny had dropped. They now saw why Angie had played this game. Kevin had his arms folded but his smile was pleasing and he nodded his approval when Angie caught his eye.

TWENTY-ONE

Sam answered the telephone. It was a call from Tony. They chatted about the weather and how Angie had been since the meeting.

'Angie...your Dad on the phone,' shouted Sam.

'Not if she's busy. I don't want to interrupt.'

'She'll be with you in a...oh, here she is I'll hand you over.'

Sam handed the phone over to his wife, as he mouthed Dad to her.

'Hi Dad. All well?' asked Angie.

'Yes, fine. Busy.'

'Busy? Up our way again?'

'No, back and forward like a weaver's shuttle between east and west. Prestonpans and Shawlands today,' said Tony.

'At least you enjoy it don't you?'

'Yes darling, it suits me fine. Pay is not bad either.'

Angie was pleased to learn more about her father. She desperately wanted this new relationship to survive.

'So have you phoned Mark yet?'

'No dad. I've been busy here and not put my mind to it yet. But I'll get round to it before long.'

'Good. I hope we can sort something out. Well must go,' he said.

'Must you, we can talk a bit more?'

'Need the loo, dear.'

'You should have gone before you dialled', chided Angie.

'I did. Bye.'

Angie reflected on their recent meeting. She wondered about his loo calls before they met and as they were leaving their meeting in Glasgow. Prostate growth was a regular feature for a middle-aged man, she knew. But it was manageable surely.

Around mid-morning a police car approached the centre. Only one policeman was in the car. He knocked on the door then asked to speak to the Director.

Angie greeted Sergeant Ralph Harkness. He was a contemporary of hers with a fresh complexion and a watch as big as Big Ben on his wrist. He stood as tall as Sam and his uniform was crisply creased. This was a man who prided himself in his appearance in uniform and in civvies too. Angie imagined he ran an impeccable home. His domestic life, in order too.

'May I have a word in private?' he requested.

'Certainly,' said Angie leading him through the centre to her room. He entered and she shut the door.

'And what brings you to our centre this morning, officer?'

'It's about one of your lads.'

'Really? Which one?'

It's Brian. He's been shoplifting.'

'And what has he been taking?'

'He took a Mars bar. You know not just one of those middle sized bars. But one of those long thick American inspired bars enough to feed a family.'

'And who did he give it to?'

'He didn't. He was seen to scoff the lot. Quite oblivious to Mrs Smart in her shop. She even had time to take a photo of him as he left. Here's a copy I ran off.'

Sergeant Harkness handed over the picture.

'It's certainly Brian,' said Angie. 'That's a surprise.'

'There's not much I can do with this case. There's no point giving it to the children's reporter. No action will be taken as he's already in care. Perhaps I should have a word with this Brian. You don't mind?

'Officer I do mind. What you have told me is the most wonderful news I've heard for several weeks.'

'Wonderful news?' asked the Sergeant screwing up his facial features.

'Yes wonderful. Brian is anorexic. Yes hard to believe. But eating a chocolate bar is such an important step in his life. Officer if you had a child who was anorexic, wouldn't you place the consumption of a chocolate over the theft to obtain it? Incidentally we shall compensate Mrs Smart financially and a letter of remorse will also be written by Brian. I shall see to that. But not a Police warning, if you don't mind.'

The Sergeant was not concentrating. His eyes were watering and his blue handkerchief received the tears. His shoulders convulsed as he tried hard to hide sobs. It was almost undignified to see the smartly dressed officer-at-law crumble before her eyes.

'Sergeant, are you all right? Have I said something....'

'No, no you give the lecture to him as you think fit...I like the idea of a ...... letter from him.'

'But I have upset you,' said Angie.

'No, no you haven't. I've upset myself. This dastardly thing anorexia. It claimed the life of our only daughter Sarah, some four years ago. It still hurts. It hurts painfully. It always will. It was when you said if you had a child who was anorexic. That got me, hit me so very hard.'

'I assure you I fully understand what you are saying and what you have experienced. I had no idea. And it's brave to face up to that tragedy. Take your time. You can stay here as long as you wish.'

'Thanks but I can't help wonder if this assessment centre had come four years ago, life would have been so different for us as a family.'

'Life might have been different, yes that's true. We can assist, help, advise and encourage but unless the victim and that's what they are, is willing to walk along the same path then it's often sad. In our short time we have lost one girl already and another is giving us great concern. She's not far off forced tube feeding.'

'I'm so pleased you are here to work with these children. And I have no problem tearing up this charge sheet. I'm sure your compensation and that letter will be sent,' said Sergeant Harkness. He stood up and gazed out of the window. His handkerchief dried his eyes and he regained his composure.

'You know at the police station my room has no view whatsoever. Here on spacious Orkney, a room with no view. What I'd pay to have this one here. You are very lucky you know.'

'We are very lucky. The children love it here and it is good to them and good for us.'

Then the loudest fart came from beneath the table. Arthur had arisen from his slumber and found the Sergeant before him. Sergeant Harkness placed his hat on the dog's head and Arthur obliged by keeping it on board. The room door was opened and Arthur was led into the hall. The children laughed at PC Arthur while Angie opened the window.

◆

Angie and Kevin interviewed Brian. He agreed to write a letter of apology but Angie wanted to know more about why he stole food. He bent his head forward and lowered his voice.

'It was Mo. I thought that's why I'm up here. I really didn't want to continue starving myself but I couldn't tell you easily.'

'Why can't you speak to us, Brian?' asked Kevin.

'It's not about you. It's what the others might think.'

'Then that's something we will have to tackle Kevin. We can't let that go on,' said Angie.

◆

That required some thought. Some plan of action. Angie would need Kevin and Lucy's support to see that obstacle removed. But as she left the centre, her thoughts turned to that telephone call to Surrey.

TWENTY-TWO

Sam viewed the televised evening news. Angie slipped through to the kitchen. She boiled the kettle and flipped a Tetley tea bag into a broad rimmed red china mug. She found a pad of paper and took a pen from behind her ear. She placed them on the counter. The boiling water scorched the bag and the colour grew darker by the second. She stirred it again before the teaspoon retrieved the bag and jettisoned it into the peelie waste bin. With a dash of milk she was ready to phone her brother.

The ring continued a few moments.

'Hello?'

'Hello, is that Gail?'

'Ah yes, it's Angie isn't it?'

'Yes. I hope you are all well?'

'You can imagine what it's like. I let the house go then when I'm expecting Mark I give it a good clean. That's what I was doing.'

'So Mark's at work nearer me than you?' asked Angie.

'Yes he's home in two days. Is it anything urgent or just a blether? I could give you his mobile number.'

Angie felt to speak to him at work on the rigs would be a distraction.

'So he's back on Friday. I'll ring him then. It can wait.'

Angie returned the receiver to its cradle. The anticlimax was not comforting. She raised her mug and tipped her tea into the sink. Perhaps another twenty four hours would clarify her thoughts even better. She returned to join Sam but the news was over and he was asleep in front of the weather forecast.

♦

When Sam woke the following morning he noticed a police van at the centre. He informed Angie.

'If it's important they'll phone me.' Before her cereal packet of shreddies was returned to the cupboard, the police van had gone. Around the side of the building an unmarked police car remained.

There was a knock on the front door. It was Sargeant Harkness. This time he wore a solemn face in greeting Sam.

'Is Dr Lawrence at home?' he enquired.

'Yes, I'll call her,' said Sam.

'No need, I'm here,' said Angie in her silent slippers. 'Come in Sergeant. Have a seat. So what brings you here so early in the day.'

'An unfortunate set of circumstances, I am afraid.'

'Really?'

'It's not about anyone in particular. It's a community thing. It has been seething under boiling point for some time. Brian's theft seems to have been the tipping point. Word got out. It was what they were expecting. You know troublesome children from Glasgow. That's what they think you have.'

'I see. So the enemy is at our back door,' said Angie.

'It's something to nip in the bud. It was somewhat inevitable. I think they have forgotten the employment your centre has brought to the island. Kitchen staff, you had plumbers and electricians and such like. But if I got the troublemakers to visit, there's a chance that they might ease off. Do you think that is possible?'

'Sergeant Harkness, it's not a zoo and they are ill children.'

'Well, unless you can come up with a better formulae the anger will ferment,' he said.

'I'll get back to you, ' Angie promised.

♦

Angie called a meeting. She informed them of the community's unrest and her reluctance to make it a nosey visit with the children trying to hide.

'We need to plan a programme,' said Kevin.

'With a strict start and finish time,' added Lucy.

'So far so good,' said Angie.

'Leave it to us Angie. We'll bring you a programme when we've created one,' said Kevin.

'Time is not on our side. The enemy are outside the gates,' said Angie. 'And they want to come in.'

♦

Two weeks later accompanied by Sergeant Harkness no less than twenty-three villagers arrived. Angie welcomed them to the Centre. She made it clear, they were able to visit any if not every room from the kitchen to the dorms and the director's office.

They would meet the children in their rooms and they could speak to them but not about their illness for these were Dr Lawrence's patients. They would return to the communal room forty five minutes later when they would be served tea and any questions would be answered.

'Welcome home, welcome home,' came from the cage.

'Oh and that's Harry the parrot. You can speak to him

too. The other member of staff you will meet is Arthur. He doesn't bite.'

The villagers politely smiled as Arthur lumbered through to sniff at skirts and trousers.

When they returned to the room the accordion was playing. Sandy was seated oblivious to the villagers who all knew him. It was symbolic of Kevin to invite Sandy back. He was one of theirs and one of the villagers too.

The children entered and sat down on the floor. Teas were served and the cook had made three cream cakes. The children served the villagers who noticed the children took none.

'This is very tasty, this cake,' said Neil Moffat the main protester. 'The kids would like it I am sure.'

'The children can have some if they want, Mr Moffat. But first children, are you ready?' asked Kevin.

The charades broke the ice. The children mimicked a gravedigger, a banker and a spaceman. Then they challenged the villagers to guess the films, Gone with the Wind; The Magnificent Seven, Mr Bean's Teddy Bear.

Sergeant Harkness took to the floor and sang in a beautiful tenor voice the Skye Boat Song. He was accompanied by Sandy and all hummed along. When encouraged to sing an encore, the Sergeant surpassed himself. It was not perhaps the most appropriate song for an adolescent gathering, but Girls Were Made to Love and Kiss was sung so sweetly. Nobody had ever heard the sergeant sing before.

The final surprise came from Lucy. She began with two of Sam's golf balls. Then each of the children threw another to her and she incorporated the ball in her juggling act. On the seventh ball disaster struck. It was one too many. The balls scattered along the room and the children were quick to retrieve them including one from Arthur's jaws. But that was done amid copious applause and laughter.

Mr Moffat rose to his feet.

'This gathering is long overdue. I tell you what we expected. Kids running amok. Kids swearing and being difficult. But I must admit, I could not have met a nicer group of children and I also appreciate the staff's organising of the entertainment.'

The gathering clapped enthusiastically.

'Don't forget the cook,' a voice shouted out.

'Oh of course not. A cake to remember thank you very much. To the juggler, the singer and musician too. A great performance and I assure you we are leaving with a very good impression of the Hazelnut Assessment Centre.'

After the applause settled down, Angie got to her feet.

'Thank you Mr Moffat. I must admit it was remiss of me not to have had an open night before today. I am glad so many of you have come. I hope you have an idea about the purpose of the centre. We have a short window of opportunity to bring lives around. When that happens it's the most wonderful achievement for the child and of course the staff. But sometimes, as recently, a child does not survive. That is why I give opportunities to each child to open up their possibilities and achieve what and when they can. Sometimes that will bring tension and anger in the community. But with a greater understanding of their needs, perhaps I can ask you to be forgiving at such times.'

Applause broke out.

'And I think that's all I need say tonight except feel free to drop by if you wish, at anytime.' Further applause rippled around the room. Harry listened with a cocked head.

'Bedtime,' he called, 'Bedtime'.

'Just before Bedtime for us all, perhaps I can thank Sandy for his support to us and Sergeant Harkness. Both men have our interest at heart and they should be applauded,' said Kevin.

And applauded they were.

'Finally to our Director Dr Lawrence who makes all things possible.'

More applause came from Kevin's request.

The gathering dispersed over the next ten minutes but the children did not leave the room. The television was switched on and Kevin arrived with a DVD film.

'Thanks one and all. You behaved very well. You made it a good evening and so I think you deserve to see this film,' said Kevin placing the DVD in the recorder.

'What film is it?' asked Sal.

'Hang on a minute,' said Kevin.

'Hang On a Minute?'

'Who's in that?' asked Colin.

'Don't be daft that's not the film's name,' said Sal.

They did not have to wait too long after some advertising trailers. But Kevin, in the meantime, read out the cover of Clockwise:

"From a script by Michael Frayn, this is a classic farce starring John Cleese as a punctilious headmaster on a calamitous journey to a conference. The plot moves along at a fair old lick, with Cleese's Mr Stimpson roping in disaffected sixth-former Laura (Sharon Maiden) to get him to his destination. There's plenty of spark to the dialogue and a very English sense of panic at the failure to meet conventional expectations. The real treat of it is Cleese's performance, its elements of priggishness ultimately overcome by sympathy at his ordeal."

One and a half hours later some very sleepy heads headed off to bed. Two were already flat out. Harry's head was sunk into its feathery neck and Arthur lay under the widow twitching as his dreams took him off on a canine journey of fantasy, almost certainly involving food.

TWENTY-THREE

She could not put it off any longer. Finding the right tone had been the issue for her. She was unsure of herself. Should she be upbeat, matter-of-fact or just downright business like? He would certainly be off duty and in Surrey now. She made a coffee and set the mug down by the receiver. Sam was engrossed in his work. As a comfort Arthur had come to her side. He accepted her patting without moving except for eyes which rolled in their sockets just in case the gratifying pats should come with fodder. She lifted the phone. She dialled with her varnished index finger. The seconds ticked by as she held her breath.

'Hello, Mark?'

'Angie dear. Great to hear you again. You well?'

'Yes, fine. And you?'

'Yea, I'm fine. So's the family. Got the grass cut today. But I love it. Having solid ground beneath me and a striped lawn devoid of any stray twigs and leaves. A contrast to the weightless North Sea operations. Magic. Pure magic. And you?'

'Oh work as usual. Lost one staff member but there's no need for me to bother you about that. I'll easily get another cook.'

'Ah, so you are not offering me a permanent post on Rousay,' laughed Mark enjoying the call.

'No, it's a rather personal matter that's on my mind. I need to share some news.'

'Yeah? Ok. I'm ready,' said Mark toning down his enthusiasm for the call. 'Hit me with it, sis.'

'Our father....' began a hesitant Angie.

'Which art in heaven...go on.' he said.

'This is serious Mark. Trust me.'

'Ok, ok sorry, I'm listening.'

'Our father served twenty six years for murdering our mother.'

'Yeah,' he confirmed.

'He's served that sentence. He lives in Glasgow and Sam bumped into him.'

'How could Sam have known it was him? And in Glasgow of all places.'

'It wasn't in Glasgow. He's got a van delivery job. He came to Kirkwall and stopped by at the Christmas Fayre. Sam was showing there. That's where they met.'

'I see,' said Mark sitting back in his chair running his free hand through his hair. He grasped a handful and pulled at it. 'God Almighty. It's true then. He's out.'

'I followed him up. I had to. We met the following week in Glasgow...'

'You actually met him? My God how could you? That man is pure evil. He killed our mother, Angie. He's a criminal. Life should mean life,' he said punching his fist on his knee.

'I know this is a surprise for you Mark...'

'Surprise? It's a bloody nightmare. Thank god I'm in Surrey...er...you didn't give him my address did you?'

'No, of course not.'

Angie knew Mark was a perfectionist. A right-winger death penalty advocate. Black was black to him. A murderer was always a murderer. She understood his stance but was disappointed.

'Mark. I don't disagree with you but he has paid his penalty to society. You can't deny him his freedom now,' she said hoping it might make him see reason.

'Paid his debt to society?..Yeah maybe...but he can never pay his debt to me or you and that's a fact. Mum's dead. I don't want to see him ever again. You hear me Angie? Never.'

'I hear you Mark. I do. But there is something else I must tell you about Mum.'

Angie recalled how Tony had reformed in prison through art. He was a new man performing a useful job in the community. Then she came to the crux of the murder. It placed some doubt in Mark's mind. If Tony was not his father, who was?

'Ok Angie. Don't let this come between us. But I assure you Tony won't be getting a Christmas card this year from me. Or any other year for that matter. Okay, got to go.'

The phone returned to its cradle but Angie held onto it. She played back the conversation in her mind. Had she forgotten anything? Arthur was at peace having dreams, unconscious of the expulsion of a foul aroma which prompted Angie to take him outside. The fresh air was good for them both. Angie continued in silence to walk slowly with him. Arthur gave a bark of contentment and Angie at that moment thought if she had another life, she'd be a Bassett hound.

Life was not a heavenly basket from which all could pilfer. Life itself owed nobody anything. She pondered these random thoughts. It was up to her to balance the needs of a father recently released and a brother who had no agenda to meet him. She was in the middle. The controlling middle she felt. Angie waited until Mark's two week home leave was over.

◆

Angie opened her mail and found a cheque floating before her eyes. It was a joint Authority maintenance grant from the sending Authorities. It was however not transferable, it had to be spent on maintenance and none was required as the building was still relatively new.

'Kevin, magnolia is like semolina,' said Angie pointing to the internal walls.

'Magnolia sells better,' he replied.

'Get the kids to chose the paint or wallpaper for their rooms. Get them to decorate their space for themselves.'

'Any restrictions?' he asked.

'You know me by now Kevin.'

'I mean financial?'

'Not at this stage. Simply get some wall paper books and some card samples, then let them decide. I'll do the maths.'

Angie went to answer the phone in her office.

'Angie dear?'

'Dad?'

'Yes, wondering how you were.'

'Not bad. Working with the kids. Sam is away to paint the Old Man of Hoy. Apart from that just honkey donkey,' she said sitting on the edge of the desk.

'Paint the Old Man of Hoy? I thought he looked just fine when I saw him when I left the island.'

'Glad you have a sense of humour Dad.'

'Ah well, not a good one. I'm no joker. Anyway, I just thought I'd let you know. Ummm...I'll have to give up the job.'

'What? Goodness me. Going for another? A full time artist perhaps?'

'If only. Angie I have to have more tests at the Beatson cancer unit.'

'Cancer? You haven't mentioned that before. Perhaps it's just a check up,' she said wracking her brain to be supportive.

'No, you've seen the signs. Frequency of loo trips. Enlarged prostate and now it's cancerous. I guess I'll be a statistic of premature death. The central Scotland health record remains intact.'

'Hey don't speak that way, Dad. You've got to stay positive.'

'Don't worry I will, but the clock is ticking. I've got six weeks at most. I won't see Easter.'

So soon after their meeting and reconciliation, it was going to end. End without a real chance of growing together.

'I'll come to see you soon, Dad. Stay strong.'

'Don't worry about me. There won't be many tears. I've not earned any.'

'Dad, that's not true. The past is past and you have a right to live. Don't say that.'

'If there's one thing I am, it's that I'm practical, Angie. It's one of the reasons I wanted to phone. You see, could you and Sam set my ashes free off Rousay?'

♦

That evening Angie telephoned Claygate. She knew Mark would not be there.

'Hello Oscar. Is Mum there?'

'I'll just get her Aunty Angie.'

It was the first time she had been called Aunty. She felt both privileged and aged. A smile played on her lips as she waited.

'Ah Gail. I hope all is well. Oscar just called me aunty and I rather like that.'

'Of course. That's what you are, sister-in-law,' replied Gail.

Angie laughed. 'Meeting your husband certainly has had its pleasing consequences.'

'So when will we see you again?' asked Gail feeling the call might be about another family gathering.

'Let's wait till the winter's over....but there again it will have to be early spring.'

'Have to? What are you planning?'

'You do have a moment for me just now?'

'Certainly,' said Gail manoeuvring a chair one handed to sit on.

'It's about Tony,' began Angie.

'Oh dear. It's really Mark you need to speak to about that. He's got no time for him, you know?'

'No one has any time for him Gail. He's dying. It's a gun at his head and one at mine too. He's probably got only six weeks, prostate cancer. I need to resolve one question. You see Tony thought Mark was the love child of Mum and another man.'

'Do you think Mark knows this?' asked Gail.

'Maybe but I doubt it. That's why I am relying on you.'

'Relying on me? How do you mean, Angie?'

'In seven weeks time we will only have doubts and feelings. We can resolve this once and for all, if you would provide some evidence.'

'Evidence? It sounds like working behind Mark's back.'

'Yes I know. It's morally wrong. I know it. It might even be illegal but what else can I do? I've given it a lot of thought, believe me and it has cried me to sleep.'

'I still think you should get Mark's permission,' said Gail.

'Yes, I should I know that. Do you think he'd want

to discuss this with me? Cos I know, he wouldn't, would he? What if DNA proved Mark is his son? Would he feel guilty? If he's not his son, then I'd not mention it again. This way we could settle the matter for you and for Mark as well as me, for once and for all time.'

'I see what you mean. I think. But doesn't that mean saliva or sperm or something you'll need like that?' asked Gail.

'It should be easier than that. Perhaps he has used a comb, perhaps you've got some dental floss of his in the bin. Can I leave that for you to find?'

'Well alright. Perhaps I'd better Google the likely sources. Mind you the bed sheets are still to be washed. Ummm...difficult to send. Leave it with me anyway, I'll get onto it immediately, before Mark gets back. But it does make me feel I'm doing something the law won't like.'

'Don't feel guilty Gail. I'm acting on Mark's behalf. It can only be positive news for him, one way or the other.'

'I see. I suppose you're right. So I post what I find to you?'

'Yes.... and I'll take it from there. Thanks Gail, I really can't do this without you. Many thanks.'

♦

Tiny pots of paint arrived and the children moved them around like chess pieces to find co-ordinating colours. Each had his or her room to decorate and the wall paper selection was studied with excitement unlike the daily school books. But soon they had made their decisions. Hazel and Zoe had gone for girly pastel pink alternating with walls of a grey/pink interlocking series of flowers. Kevin noticed Hazel's artistic appreciation and that had attracted Zoe, so the girls rooms would be identical. Nick had gone for a space theme with rockets and planets on all four walls with a request for a black ceiling. Silver stars floated in his sky. Billy had his favourite football team in mind. Green and white peppermint stripes on the door. The first wall gave his allegiances away without looking at the other three walls showing Parkhead with a goal being scored against Motherwell.

Angie was delighted with their selections except those of Colin. His was a black ceiling and black walls except for one which he wanted to leave blank. Magnolia and black did not meet with her complete approval and she told Kevin.

'But it's what he wants,' said Kevin.

'Of course,' she replied.

TWENTY-FOUR

Angie feared the worst when she arrived back at the centre. A hand written message awaited her. It required her to telephone a local number on her return from Kirkwall. Angie was prepared to defend any complaint that might be heading her way as the result of the activities of one or a group of the children. She dialled.

'Is that Dr Lawrence?'

'Yes, speaking.'

'Good afternoon dear. I do hope you don't mind me calling. I'm Betty Nicolson. Just up the road from you. You see I have a piano which has not had a finger on its keys for some time now. I wonder if...you would like to take it?'

'That sounds a great idea. Where do you live?'

'Not far away. I can see your centre from my lounge. I'm at Brae's Knowe on the B 9064.'

'I know where you are. Well, shall I arrange a removal van at your convenience?'

'I don't think that's necessary. I've already got it on runners. It just glides along. Perhaps a few of your youngsters could help?'

'Will you be in tomorrow morning? Let's say 11am?'

'Excellent. I'll see you then.'

'Thank you very much indeed. Now to find a youngster with muscles,' Angie laughed.

♦

Sam had the windows wide open as Angie entered her home that evening. The smoke alarm went off.

'You ok Sam?' she enquired as she quickly hung up her coat.

'Bloody lamb chops. That fire alarm is too sensitive.'

Angie relaxed. Panic over. She entered the kitchen. Sam stood before the grill with oven gloves ready to rescue the chops. She gave him a bear hug.

'You can never be too sensitive.'

'Change. The meal will be on the table in two minutes,' said Sam.

'Ok I'm on my way.'

They sat at the table with Arthur settled underneath resting his head on Angie's foot.

'Have I got a surprise for you?' asked Angie.

'Oh dear, what are you up to?'

'Nothing sinister. Remember in your teenage years what you did as a hobby?'

'Bird watching....'

'No not so academic...'

'My bird watching skills were fine tuned. How else could I have chosen you.'

'Ha ha Sam. No, you were in a band weren't you?'

'Yup played jazz keyboard.'

'Well tomorrow the centre will acquire a piano. Isn't that great?'

'Good grief I've not played for years now.'

'Surely it's like riding a bicycle?'

'You mean once learnt never forgot?'

'Yea,' she said.

'It's more like golf. If you give that up, you're rubbish next time out. But will it be in the Centre?'

'Yea but that shouldn't stop you.'

'Oh by the way are you sure you've given up sending yourself presents?'

'You know I have,' said Angie lowering her voice to a whisper. Why bring that sore point up again she thought.

'Well that jiffy bag came today. It's for you.'

Angie placed her knife and fork down and stood up. Arthur was disturbed. He came from underneath the table wagging his tail. She lifted the brown jiffy and pulled back the flap. Inside was a white square cardboard box. Inside the box was a short note. She read it to Sam.

'I hope I've come up trumps, Mark's toenail enclosed. Love Gail.'

'Woopeee..wonderful. It's a great start,' she said.

'What the dickens do you need Mark's toenail for. It is a fetish?' asked Mark.

'No, don't be daft,' she replied.

'Me daft? It's not me. What the hell do want with your brother's toenail? Not an unreasonable question to ask, surely?'

'It could have been a hair from his comb. But this is much better. I need to see if Dad's DNA matches with Tony's.'

Sam reflected for a moment on the underhand machinations of a distorted family.

'Hang on a minute. Mark wants nothing to do with his alleged father you told me and you are trying to prove otherwise. Let sleeping dogs lie Angie. What good can this possibly do? In fact I doubt if this is legal.'

'I told you, Tony's only got a few weeks left. What if Mark finds out that Tony is his father after he's dead? How do you think he'd feel?'

'You are out of my depths Angie. It's all beyond me. It seems you found bliss in finding your brother and now you are risking losing him forever.'

'Trust me Sam, trust me.'

♦

Kevin was in charge of team of three who walked to Mrs Nicolson's door the following day. Troy, Brian and Colin were the only volunteers. As they approached her home, the garage was open and the piano was secure sitting on two brackets each having four wheels at the front and back.

'Good morning Mrs Nicholson. I'm Kevin Mensah, a psychologist at the centre. We've got a team of our three muscled men.'

The boys laughed.

'This is a very kind offer Mrs Nicolson. You are sure you want it removed?' asked Kevin.

'There comes a time when things like this are in better hands. And I hope it will give the children a chance to learn something about music.'

'I'm sure it will. And if the windows are open and the wind is from the North West, I guess you'll hear them playing. So boys, no mistreating this piano.'

'Just before you go gentlemen. Do come in. I've got some juice for you. And Mr Mensah tea or coffee?'

'Thank you very much. This is very kind of you. Boys, this way..oh and a coffee if I may,' said Kevin.

On a white lace tablecloth was a collection of tumblers with large bottles of Fanta and Pespsi Cola. Lying before them was a plate of freshly made pancakes with melting butter restrained by luscious strawberry jam. Mrs Nicholson had obviously made a great effort to please.

'Boys, help yourselves,' said Mrs Nicholson turning to the kitchen to boil the kettle.

Only Colin took a pancake and he made sure Troy and Brian were missing something special. Colin took another.

'This is very thoughtful of you Mrs Nicholson,' said Kevin

'Oh nothing really. When I had a family I knew how to win their hearts making pancakes,' she replied.

Kevin spread the strawberry jam on his pancake leaving some of the confiture on his fingers. He licked them clean.

'Mr Mensah. I have another instrument for you perhaps, in the attic. It was one my late husband enjoyed playing but it's not for me. Do you think the boys would be interested in a.. um ..I think..... It's a tenor saxophone?' she said.

Kevin's eyes lit up.

'I can teach the saxophone,' he said.

'You mean you can play it?' she enquired.

Kevin smiled and nodded.

'One moment please,' she said climbing the stairs.

Mrs Nicolson came down with a long black box. Kevin own saxophone was in his parental home in Giffnock in Glasgow. He took hold of the box and unzipped three sides. He took out the main part of the instrument and slipped the ribbon holder over his head. He inserted the top piece and then the reed fitted snugly in its mouthpiece holder. Kevin took a breath. Note perfectly he played Sleepy Shores then on the second verse he jazzed up the theme and played as if he was a sand pipit flirting here and there along the shore. He played as if possessed, his feet tapping and his shoulders rising on the high notes. His puffed out cheeks made the music loud but he did not lose his tune. When he came to a finish all three boys were in the kitchen with their mouths open. Colin's still had strawberry jam on his teeth. When Kevin ended he finished off his cool coffee.

The boys insisted that Kevin play as the piano set off along the flat road. When a car passed by it did so when the piano stopped but the saxophone carried on playing. The driver tooted as he passed. His note was out of key. Only one other vehicle passed on their progress to the centre. It was a tractor.

Kevin supervised the piano's proximity to the verge. The big wheeled tractor sped by as if the driver had not noticed the strange gathering of itinerant musicians. When they reached the centre, more interest was shown in the saxophone than the piano until Sam arrived. Sam sat down to play. First he warmed his fingers up by playing consecutive key scales. Then he looked at Kevin and nodded in a four beat count. He played Sweet Georgia Brown. Kevin quickly joined in and all the centre staff and children gathered to listen to the unexpected talent in their midst. Only one saw little purpose in the activity. Arthur realised this intrusive thing, music, had nothing to do with food. But he lay across Elly's seated legs which stamped out the rhythm of the traditional jazz. All enjoyed the impromptu concert but one person was missing. Her train was approaching Glasgow Queen Street Station.

♦

Angie gave her father a hug. She noticed his face was gaunter. His step slower and his beard had grown at least one or two days without a shave.

'Come on let's go for a Costa coffee.'

They walked arm in arm out through the station. They passed a café selling coffee.

'Won't this one do?' asked Tony.

'I'm in the mood for a Costa, there's one not far away,' she replied.

'Coffee was always the same when I was inside. Coloured dishwater. Tea was a bit better especially with no milk or sugar. They used a tea bag and if I was lucky, I got it on the first ducking.'

'These days are over Dad. You've got to make each day special from now on.'

They found a Costa shop and sat inside out of the cold. Angie brought over the drinks together with a Cinnamon bun and a Chelsea bun.

'Your choice,' she said.

'No, it's yours Angie. Ladies choice. I've not said that for a very long time.'

Angie took the Chelsea bun and passed the Cinnamon one over to her father.

'There you go again. Talking about the past. It's the future we need to talk about.'

'At times I think I only have a past. And now I've not got a future. Darling, this may be our last meeting,' he said staring into Angie's eyes.

She began to feel tears well up. Tony placed his hands over hers. 'Angie there's one thing I want to say. When I'm gone, I want to be cremated.'

'Ok,' said Angie regaining her composure. 'Have you made a will?'

'I'm seeing a lawyer later this week. We will have to work from scratch. That's sharpened my focus. You are my only relative. Will you spread my ashes on Rousay, on the beach or in the sea, I don't mind?'

Angie held his arm. 'Of course dad. Anything you want.'

Tony lifted his coffee and finished it with one last gulp. 'Excuse me,' he said. 'The troubles again.'

When Tony was away, Angie took off the lid from which Tony had drunk his tea and placed it in a brown envelope which already contained the white box. She placed it in her bag and covered it up. She almost finished her coffee as Tony returned but she took her lid and fitted it over his cup. Holding the two cups as one, she stood up.

'So where to now?' he asked.

'George Square. Let's feed the pigeons.'

As they left, Angie placed the two paper mugs with one top in the Costa bin satisfied that Tony had not noticed her subtle subterfuge.

The friendly pigeons accepted Angie's well travelled cheese sandwiches. When they came to an end Tony placed his arm around Angie as they sat in the square.

'You know I could have been wrong about Mark. I'm glad that he's done well for himself, in fact pleased that you have both done so well. But I'll go to my rest not knowing about him and that's best. We'll not meet and he'll not enquire about me. His mind is at rest. Mine is too. Let's leave it that way.'

'It seems you are resigned to the inevitable.'

'Yes dear. When the band starts to play, you have to dance to the music,' he said.

'Give me a ring when you think you have sorted out everything, you know, the will, your affairs.'

'I've started to clear out the flat. I'm stopping the rent at the end of the month.'

'Is that wise?'

'Advised by my consultant. Or was it the Marie Curie? Anyway I'll be at the Beatson from then on.'

'Do you mind if I can ask about funeral costs.'

'No, they discussed that too. I'll be able to pay that, don't worry, and I'll have a little left. Not much mind you, but it will be yours. You might even get another Costa coffee out of it,' he laughed. So did Angie. Black humour deserves a belly laugh she knew but her laugh was couched in sorrow.

They had a meal at the Via Italia where the spaghetti and fettuccini tangled on their forks. The Garganega wine was consumed and the profiteroles with Italian ice cream completed the tasty meal. Tony tried hard to pay.

'No Tony, this is on me.'

Angie was to board the train to Aberdeen so they parted at George Square to go their own ways after a tearful hug. Tony stood by the bus stop for Great Western road. Angie called into a nearby post office with her parcel and had it weighed.

'Yes, first class please,' she demanded.

TWENTY-FIVE

The first plane from Aberdeen to Kirkwall touched down at 9.30am the next day. Sam was there to meet his wife with a kiss and a warm embrace.

'How was Tony?'

'He's losing weight and ending his flat rent.'

'Is that wise?' asked Sam.

'Consultant's advice.'

'So he's not got long,' said Sam taking Angie's bag to the car.

'No but I've got the samples off.'

Sam shook his head from side to side. But Angie saw a smile on his lips as he did. The car set out from Kirkwall on the homeward leg. It was a bright morning with a mild feeling. Ideal for photography but that was not on Sam's mind.

'There's been some developments on the campus Ma'am.'

'What are you talking about?'

'It turns out Hazel can play the old Joanna. She reached grade five before the weight daemon crept in. She kept up with Kevin on sax.'

'Kevin on sax. Wow and did Hazel enjoy playing?' asked Angie.

'Enjoy playing? I've never seen that girl smile as much.'

'That's good. And Kevin, a saxophone? Where did that come from?'

'Mrs Nicolson was clearing out so the sax made its journey over too. Kevin led the way from the house playing with the piano on wheels following. What a sight.'

'Who was pulling the piano?'

'Hardly pulling. It's a very flat road. Troy, Brian and Colin went with him,' said Sam.

'Brian? That was a mistake. He'll be put on rest for the remainder of the day.'

'What, I don't get this CTB....

'You mean CBT Cognitive Behaviour Therapy.'

'Ok CBT. It seems to me you're damned if you do and damned if you don't. I mean, does the fact that he was chosen and he agreed and he joined with two others in a visit to a normal home, ate a pancake and drank juice then guided the piano back on a flat road, not count as a good positive experience?'

'I didn't know about the pancake and juice.'

Sam drummed his fingers on the steering wheel. He stared ahead as the road slipped under the bonnet. Angie placed her hand on his thigh and gently rubbed it.

'Each to their own. How's the Old Man coming along?'

'You interested?'

'Yeah.'

'Well, I'm fine,' he said.

'Not you dafty. Your Old Man of Hoy?'

'I've completed the sketch.'

♦

Four days later a letter marked Strictly Confidential and Private landed on the carpet. Sam placed it on the dining room table. It would await Angie's return that evening.

♦

In the afternoon Kevin took all the pupils to the Loch of Wabister, three miles from the centre. He supervised them on two long rowing boats suitably attired in luminous life jackets. Those who wished, dropped worms on hooks into the water. It was exciting as they held their lines, anticipating the first nibble. Their excitement became audible.

'Schhhh' said Kevin. 'You don't want to frighten them away.'

'I've got one, I've got one. Let's get the line up, quick,' said Troy.

The line was pulled up very quickly and the expected weight diminished.

'Fuck, it got away,' he said.

The others laughed at his bad luck.

'Fix another worm then and this time take your time. Pull the line up slowly. Tire the fish out,' said Kevin.

They fished for two hours and brought back four brown trout of a reasonable size, two rainbow trout and a pike. When the boats were back on the shore of the loch, Kevin marched them back to the centre where Arthur gave them a particularly warm welcome. That night fish was on the menu and the cook did them proud. Baked in foil with a sprinkling of lemon and melted butter with chopped herbs containing parsley and basil and a few sliced almonds, Arthur's nose was alert to the unexpected aroma but Angie was back at her home with a similar nose for fish.

'Hmmm that smells good. What are you cooking Sam?'

'Kevin dropped by with a brown trout. A good four pounder so that's what we're having with new potatoes and green beans.'

'Cool. Down soon.'

Sam opened a bottle of Californian Elk Cove Pinot Gris white wine from Oregon. Angie re-appeared two minutes later having changed, all but her Ecco Mules of course.

'What's the special, occasion then?' she enquired as she entered the dining room.

'To a happy customer,' said Sam as they clinked their glasses together.

'And who might that be?'

'Angus e-mailed me asking how I was getting on. So I took a photo of the sketch of The Old Man and sent it as an attachment.'

'Hmm...so he likes it so far?'

'He was pleased with what he saw and how it was coming along.'

'Bloody hell...'

'What's up Sam?'

'Buddy fith bom in the roof ob ma mouf.'

'Got it out?' she asked.

With his fingers pinched Sam retrieved the bone. He placed it on the lip of the plate.

'Wow that was not nice. I hope you have better news in that envelope,' said a recovering Sam.

Angie cleaned her plate, leaving the skin and tail at the plate lip.

'There are some currant scones in the bread bin. Let's have one with a cup of tea. I'm going to the settee. I'll read this there.'

With the confidential warnings on the envelope Angie had no doubt about what the letter would contain. She took her comb from her handbag and neatly inserted it at the top of the letter. She tugged gently and the envelope opened showing a white sheet of paper. Angie took it out. She turned it the right way round and read the preamble. There were clear warnings if this information was taken without the subject's approval then it would not be acceptable in a court of law. But Angie needed the secrets of the family to resolve the past. She turned over the page and saw the result of two tests. Both showed that Mark was the son of Tony. Angie's lips did not know whether to smile or frown. It was news that Mark would not welcome easily and Tony's guilt would be doubled at a time his life was edging away.

◆

The children enjoyed the freedom they had been given to paint their rooms. As each child thought through his or her future, they could do so from a sound base in which their maturity was coming into focus. Angie was pleased to see Billy's weight increase coinciding with him becoming one of the most popular of mates. Elly who spent much time with Harry on her arm, remained her most worrying child. Her weight gain was nil and the hair on her arms had started to show more prominently. The truancy issues had gone primarily as they were isolated and they were fast approaching the sixteen age barrier after which education would not be compulsory but Angie had received good school class reports of her clients from their resident teacher.

'Brush brush brush,' said Harry sitting on his perch.

'Hello Harry,' said Elly.

'Hello, hello, hello,' replied the precocious bird.

'Do you love me?'

'I love you,' replied Kofi.

'Kofi loves everyone, Elly. Not just you,' said Brian.

'Anyone can do that. Kofi do you love me?' teased Brian.

Kofi bent forward straining his neck towards the lad.

'Go tae hell; go tae hell', he said nodding his head up and down.

Elly laughed loudly. Others joined in.

'Serves you right Brian, you taught him to say that yourself,' said Colin.

♦

When Angie returned home, Sam informed her there had been a call from Glasgow. She had to phone back immediately.

'Oh that'll be dad. I'll do it soon,'

'No it's not his number Angie. It's the Beatson Cancer unit.'

TWENTY-SIX

Still in her work clothes, Angie dialled the Glasgow number. She waited a few minutes.

'Beatson Hospital here, Gwen speaking.'

'Ah can I speak to the clinical nurse, Miss Ruth Burns please?'

'One moment please.'

One moment lingered on to two minutes before the connection was made.

'Hello, Dr Lawrence? Sorry to keep you waiting. I was with a patient.'

'That's understandable. You asked me to phone back.'

'That's right. You are the next of kin and so I needed to speak to you. Your father Tony Arnold, is not at all well. He's slipping into unconscious moments.'

'Is he in pain?' asked Angie.

'No, never pain. We ensure that. That's why he's here. Prostate cancer is in Tony's case metastatic. Sadly it has spread considerably. A younger man might have responded to chemotherapy or drugs but Tony's PSA; that's the Prostate Specific Antigen is taken regularly. That simply confirmed the worst fear. Tony's cancer is aggressive. It's advanced.'

'I see. Then he does not have long to live?'

'Exactly. That's why I needed to speak to you.'

'Do you have an idea....I mean...,' struggled Angie to find the right words to say.

'How long he has got to live?' suggested Nurse Burns.

'Yes.'

'That's never an exact science of course but with my years of experience with patients such as your father, I'd say only two or three days perhaps.'

'That quick?'

'Yes, if you could come and see him the sooner the better, although you might still find him unconscious.'

Angie talked through the conversation she had with Nurse Burns. Sam listened carefully as he dried his hands after washing up the dishes.

'Well you'll have to get down there as soon as you can. I'd like it to be both of us.'

'I'd appreciate that Sam.' Angie's mind was racing like a spinning top out of control. She looked in her purse where she had placed Mark's card.

Angie dialled his mobile number. She could not wait to call him, whatever he might be doing.

'Angie?'

'Yes, is it convenient? I mean you are not disappearing into the sea in the dark are you?'

'I have to sometimes at night but not tonight. I'm in the mess finishing a meal,' he said with his phone trapped between his neck and his collar bone.

'Do you want me to phone back?'

'No Angie, it's ok. Carry on.'

'Perhaps it is a more personal than social chat,' she said biting her bottom lip.

'Ok let me phone back. I'll go to my cabin. Be in touch in five.'

Angie replaced the telephone.

'He'll phone back in a few minutes Sam. I suppose I'll just have to wait.'

'Want a G&T in the meantime?'

'A small one then,' she said as she stretched her arms

over her head, took a deep breath and draped her hands over the nape of her neck.

'God, I'm scared. ' She paced the room back and forward.

'It's just got to be done and you know it. Here, take your glass,' said Sam catching up on her. The phone rang.

'Hi sorry about that. Much quieter now. So you've something to tell me?' asked Mark.

'Yes. The Beatson Cancer care hospital has been in touch. Tony has only a day or so to live,' she said.

'I see. So you want me to patch things up, before it's too late sort of thing.'

'Mark, Tony is unconscious he's not up to discuss anything. But you are right it would be a last chance to see him.'

'Last chance? It would be the first. But if he's not my father, why should I bother?'

'Then he's your step-father.'

'A stepfather I've never known and never liked,' said Mark. 'You go ahead and see him out. Don't let this come between us Angie. Count me out.'

'If I said he was your father would it make any difference?'

Mark's hesitation gave Angie some hope.

'Sure it would, if he was my father but don't forget he killed our mother. Remember I was the family bastard and God knows who my real father might have been.'

Angie heard Mark take a deep breath as he considered what had been said. He seemed vulnerable after all.

'Let's say he is your father. Will you come down with me to visit him?'

Mark was now struggling to hold his tears back. Could he let his sister down? Did it really matter if Tony was not conscious. But above all Mark knew it was a last chance to see the man who just might have been his father.

'Ok. When are you going down?' asked Mark.

'I was thinking I could take off tomorrow to get down and back the next day. If I flew down from Kirkwall and you flew from Aberdeen, we could meet at Glasgow airport. How does that sound.'

'Can we hold off for a few minutes? I might be able to make you a better offer.' They hung up.

'Well, that could have been worse,' said Sam relieved that the call was over.

'Yea but it's not clarified anything and there's no delay in booking a flight.'

'Wait till Mark calls back. He seems a very resourceful, feet-on-the-ground sort of chap.'

'Yes, he is,' said Angie sipping her drink. 'But Mark still doesn't seem to acknowledge that he's Tony's son.'

Twenty five minutes later Mark rang back.

'Ok Tomorrow morning 9am at your place. We set off together. Be there by mid-day and set off home again at 7pm. How does that sound?'

'From my place?'

'Yes, just like last time. We found a safe landing nearby.'

'So we're going by helicopter,' said Angie.

'Yes. A stinking, oily, noisy helicopter but it will save lots of time,' said Mark.

TWENTY-SEVEN

The whir of the helicopter announced its presence out of a clear blue sky. It descended over flecks of white waves which appeared, then were lost beneath the sea, stolen by King Neptune.

Spiv landed the aircraft on the same position as before and Mark ran from the plane to greet Angie and Sam as they left their front door.

'Glad you're well wrapped up. There's no central heating aboard,' said Mark. 'I should have told you.'

'We've got each other,' laughed Angie.

As they ran to the craft, eyes appeared from the glass windows waving at them as they passed by. Kevin waved with one hand, his other was holding a letter close to his heart.

Angie and Sam were pulled into the metal frame but Spiv told them they would be going nowhere until a flock of gulls moved away.

'There's just too many for safety,' he said.

Angie took out her mobile.

'Is it all right to make a call just now? I mean it won't interfere with the mechanics?' Spiv nodded his permission.

'Kevin, get the kids out to scare off the gulls. We cannot take off till they've dispersed.'

Spiv closed his fist and his thumb rose up as he saw the children running and shouting towards the lazy gulls. Aggressive and bold gulls could hold their own and especially in numbers but with the swirling propellers, the approaching children and a Basset Hound bringing up the rear, a three pronged attack was more than they could stomach. The helicopter lifted as soon as the gulls had left.

'You know Sam. I've never met a real artist before,' said Mark.

Sam smiled as he contemplated a response to his newly found brother-in-law.

'I'm an artist yes, but a child too. I see things differently. I cannot pass a hedge without seeing a variety of greens in the foliage. I can stare at clouds for ages seeing them change in shape and in velocity wondering how I can catch them in a moment of time. I guess you all see the big picture. I see the miniature. It's about seeing the world a different way,' shouted Sam above the din of the engines. Mark nodded as if he had taken in all the nuances of his craft. Anyway, he got the gist of his erudition.

Land came up to meet the helicopter as it passed over the Monadhliath Mountain (2702 feet) west of the snow covered Cairngorms. During the flight Angie realised the sooner Mark was told the truth the better. She was prepared to meet the flak from such a height. She placed her hand on Mark's knee and bent forward. He then placed his hand on her hand as he leant forward.

'Mark, Tony is your Dad,' said Angie.

'What?' he replied as he digested her statement screwing his eyes close.

'I said Tony is your Dad.'

'How do you know?'

'Because I did a DNA test. It confirmed you are his son.'

Mark sat back for a moment wondering how this could have happened.

'How did you do it?' he asked.

'I got a coffee cup trace from Dad.'

'Ok, but how did you get it from me?'

'I pressurized Gail,' said Angie.

'What do you mean?' he asked.

'I had to get the answer before Tony died. You would not have accepted the truth after he had died. So she gave me a toe nail clipping.'

'I didn't know about that.'

'No, you were at sea. But don't blame Gail. I just had to get something to compare your DNA to his.'

'You could have asked me,' he suggested.

'Really Mark?' said Angie with a smile and a shake of her head.

Mark began to smile. He realised the truth. He would never have agreed and it showed his sister was her own woman. A determined girl who in retrospect, had made the right decision.

'That puts a different perception on Tony for me,' said Mark.

'Me too. Whatever sort of mother and father we had, we are their children,' said Angie leaving Mark to contemplate a new reality.

'Well, perhaps the truth needed to surface,' he said eventually.

'The truth is, we're family, Mark.'

Spiv pointed to a garden on top of a long building, in a built-up part of Glasgow.

'That's the Beatson,' he said.

The helicopter found sufficient flat land to descend onto the Botanical Gardens in Great Western road. Mark, Angie and Sam left the helicopter and took a taxi to the Beatson while Spiv stayed around to prevent any over-inquisitive Glaswegian visitors.

Although the 2008 building looked modern, the Beatson had been in place two centuries ago and each year it had learned more of cancerous causes, issues, treatment and support. They now offered the most caring environment with the latest technology to attack the daemon cancer.

They were led along a long corridor by a MacMillan Nurse who spoke of Tony being dependent on morphine. They would find him weak. Room 7 was all but one room from the end of the corridor.

'I see he's in a room by himself,' Angie stated.

'Yes, it's appropriate at this stage, for him and his family,' said the nurse.

They found Tony lying on his pillow with his mouth open but he was asleep.

'Tony.....Dad...' said Angie. 'I've got Sam and Mark with me today.

Tony gave an apparent smile but his eyes remained closed. Angie held his hand and looked up at her husband then brother. She shook her head as if to say, he wasn't acknowledging anyone.

'Tony, Sam here. Are you having forty winks?' he asked in a louder voice. But Tony did not move.

Mark approached and held his hand. He then gently stroked his forehead. 'I'm your son Mark,' he said. Tony opened his eyes and his smile grew larger.

'M.....Mark....my son....and Angie....my daug....' but the end of the word fell from his lips into an inaudible whisper. Mark held on as his eyes shut. Angie went to find the nurse.

'Nurse, it's about my father. Can you tell me, does he ever gain full conscience?'

Nurse Burns took her arm and led her to a seat in her office.

'Less in these hours, much less. He has not long to live. I gather you came from Orkney?'

'Yes, that's right.'

'Well, you can stay the night here if you wish. There's

no charge. There's accommodation only two doors down the corridor.'

'We came by helicopter and will be returning later this evening,' said Angie.

'Well, perhaps if you could stay for the next hour or so,' she said.

'Yes, we could. Er...at the end of his bed....?'

'Tony's notes you mean? They are clear to read. The amount of morphine he is having is to calm the rage of the cancer throughout his body. He can't take much more. I don't think he'll make it through this evening,' she said.

Angie returned to the room and met with Mark and Sam in a huddle. She informed them of what the nurse said. Tony lay motionless, his eyes as closed as the cell of his former jail. Sam set off to find a tray of teas and biscuits. He did not travel far. He met the nurse who said he should leave it in her hands. When he returned he noticed Mark had taken a camera from his pocket.

'Here, let me take a shot of you beside your father.'

Angie bent over at one side. She remained while Mark stood on the other side. Sam found the focus. Then Sam stood at the end of the bed for a shot of the artist he discovered then he took separate shots of his wife and his brother-in-law with Tony. In fact he took eight pictures in all. He handed the camera back to Mark.

'It's a pity these photos are the last of a lifetime of photos but at least this will give you one memory.'

'Thanks Sam. Thanks,' smiled Mark as he put his camera away.

The tray arrived. The clatter of plates, cups and saucers made a din but did not cause any movement from Tony.

'Pity we can't share this with Spiv,' said Angie.

'I know Spiv. No doubt a kid has come to see the helicopter and he's got him to bring him a hot cup of tea and a sausage roll. A handsome tip would come his way no doubt,' said Mark.

Half an hour later after the tray had been removed, the nurse returned. She took Tony's pulse. She rested her hand on his brow and lifted an eyelid. Finally she positioned the back of her hand by his nose. She turned to smile at them.

'In your presence, Tony has slipped away. I offer my condolences to you all.'

Angie stood up and thanked the nurse. She approached her father and kissed his still warm lips. Sam followed and laid his hands on Tony's hands. He patted them twice then made way for Mark. Mark hesitated. Tears were in his eyes.

'Let's go. Yes, let's go now,' he said.

TWENTY-EIGHT

In late March despite much snow lying around on higher ground, the days were getting longer and bright sunny days followed in a glorious sequence of five at a time. It gave Sam an additional spurt to his work and the Old Man of Hoy was completed. All that was left was to find an appropriate picture frame and then post it to London.

The centre was at full capacity despite the departures of Billy, Troy, Nick and Brian. Additional beds were taken up by children from Cumbria as well as Glasgow, Paisley, Dumfries and Dundee. Arthur took new feet in his stride and rewarded newcomers with his attention and antics. Lucy was now worth her weight in gold having gained confidence in her reformed duties. With each new intake she was popular and always ready to lend a hand or provide a shoulder for tears. Harry never forgot the profanities he had been taught and was ready to learn more to entertain the children while he played his part in giving the muted speakers the confidence to speak again.

Kevin had completed his placement and Angie had given him a glowing report. He would graduate in Glasgow University's Bute Hall in May. Angie had received an invitation to attend the ceremony. She had also invited him to take on full employment at the centre on Rousay but he declined. He wrote that he wanted to be near his partner and so their wedding would be in Glasgow before the year was out. He did say that they might come back to see everyone before then. Angie was quick to be in touch with Edinburgh and Glasgow University to offer placements again and she had been fortunate. Two female Doctorate students would be arriving after Easter. This time she would inspect their credentials in greater detail.

Angie sat on the settee with her legs crossed. One socked foot rubbed the other itchy ankle. She ran through her contacts on her mobile.

'Hi Mark, tell me. The long range weather forecast looks like we could spread Tony's ashes to the Atlantic in the second week of April. How does that sound?'

'You believe in weather forecasts?' asked Mark.

'Why, don't you?'

'Bracing, I'd say but if that suits you, I'll be there. No need for Gail to come though. She'll have the kids to look after and of course she never knew Tony. So you set the date. Either a Friday or Saturday suits me. Best if I came from the rig.'

'Fine. Okay take care and love to Gail and the kids,' said Angie switching off.

◆

Two weeks later Mark, Sam and Angie boarded the Harvest Store at Kirkwall as Sandy Flett had met Sam again and heard of the plans to scatter his father-in-law's ashes.

The boat headed out of the Bay of Kirkwall, past Puldrite Skerry, a mere dimple in the water. It kept to the port side of Gairsay when the waters grew choppier. An inquisitive common seal approached hoping some fish entrails might be coming its way but Sandy had ensured his sons had the Harvest Store looking its best for this solemn occasion. The decks had been thoroughly washed down and around the wheelhouse was pinned a sash of black material fluttering in the wind but remained intact.

Angie appreciated what Sandy had done. Sam knew not to question the tradition of the Orkney funeral at sea and Mark just felt it a bit ostentatious but held his tongue.

Sam held on tight to the bar in front of the wheelhouse as the boat rose and fell out of step with his stomach. He was as pale as the shores he often painted but his eyes were not studying this seascape. Sandy saw that he was not himself and passed him a large paper cup. Sam took it gratefully and moments later filled it. Sandy motioned for him to throw the biodegradable cup overboard and Sam felt much better when he did.

The spray was fine and salty. Ideal for a brown paper wrapping of fish and chips. Once more they took the port side, this time off Egilsay sailing close to Mae Ness. Angie held Tony's ashes on her lap, somewhat surprised that the Twiglets tin which contained his last remains was so heavy. Her hands caressed the tin. Mark who was more of a seaman, at least used to the vagrancies of the North Sea, stood on the prow of the ship with his own thoughts.

Beyond Kili Holm they saw the Faraclett Head and they knew they were in the Westray Firth and about to turn into Saviskaill Bay. As they saw the centre and their old stone cottage, Sandy killed the engine and only the gulls and arctic terns could be heard questioning why the boat had stopped. It drifted a little and Sandy came out of the wheel house.

'Here's a good spot. You can see it from your home and the current will take the ashes out to the Atlantic and God knows where after that. Mind you some might just drift towards the shore.'

From his pocket Sam produced a table spoon. He gave it to Angie.

'I was just going to tip half of it in and leave the rest for Mark,' she said.

'With the spoon you can spread them more often and have more thoughts of your father whose tragic life came together up here in Orkney,' reminded Sam.

Angie felt that an appropriate gesture and rewarded Sam with a brief kiss.

Mark and Angie stood together at the bow. Angie knelt to keep her balance from the bobbing waves. Then in silence she took the first spoonful. She flicked it forward but some of the light ash took off on the wind across the sea.

'Perhaps Tony wants to fly like me,' said Mark.

'Maybe,' said Angie. She continued with another half dozen spoonfuls of ash before handing the tin over to Mark.

Mark completed the ceremony and closed the lid of the tin. Sandy stepped forward between the siblings and opened a glass bottle of Talisker whisky. He leant over the boat and emptied half the bottle into the sea.

My god, what a waste thought Mark.

'There you go Tony. I never kent you but it's our traditional way to see you off well. Ah now don't you worry, I've left some over for us.' Sandy produced three mugs and dribbled the remains out equally.

'Slange Ava,' said Sandy.

'Slange Ava' they replied in chorus as they raised their mugs to the waves.

'Sam see on the beach. Two folk. That must be Kevin and his fiancée.'

Angie waved towards the beach. A second or two later, the couple responded with their waves.

'Yes, it must be. They'll surely wait till we get back,' Angie said looking at her wrist watch.

It took fifty minutes to return to Kirkwall where Sam had parked the car. Sam was particularly pleased to be on dry hard land again and his hand shook Sandy's with gratitude for a safe return as much as his thoughtfulness in helping the family carry out Tony's last wishes. Angie slipped him a wodge of notes.

'Oh away with you. We look after each other out here in the islands. That's what it's aboot. Here, take it back.'

'No, I really must insist. It's for your petrol then.'

'No Angie. It's no petrol anyway. It's diesel these engines we've got but you can make better use of the money with your kids up there. I insist.'

As they drove back in the car, they felt they had completed a satisfying ceremony.

'In Surrey no one refuses cash. It's a different money grabbing culture down there,' said Mark.

'Aye that's what I like about living up here. Not just the scenery for my art but the down to earth people, the salt of the earth. They may baulk at modern society but their roots are solid in the grounds of these islands. And as our first year is almost up, I guess we've gained quite a few friends outside the centre,' said a fully recovered Sam. The car drew up to the cottage as the visitors left the centre and began to approach the Lawrence household.

'It's definitely Kevin but he's not brought his fiancée, it's a man. Perhaps he's a psychologist wanting a job. Sam, put the kettle on.'

Mark straightened the cushions and made the lounge look presentable as the kettle bubbled in the kitchen. Angie had time to make a quick loo break.

'Hello,' said Kevin entering the open door.

'Dr Kevin Mensah, I think it is now isn't it?' asked Mark.

'Sounds strange. It was Dr Lawrence when I was last here and I was the gofer. Mind you I certainly haven't got her experience yet,' said Kevin.

'Nonsense, you've had as much experience as is needed Kevin,' said Angie appearing from the bathroom and heading straight to give Kevin a welcome kiss and cuddle.

'Now introductions please. Tell me about the new psychologist,' asked Angie looking at the man who had still to make his voice heard.

'Oh, you mean Gordon. He's not a psychologist. He's a market gardener,' said Kevin as Gordon came forward to shake everyone's hand. As he did so Kevin clarified the situation.

'Gordon and I are engaged. We'll have our wedding in September. You are all invited.'

'Ohh...I see....It will be my first gay wedding,' said Angie instinctively yet amazed that she hadn't seen any signs of his homosexuality.

'Errr...mine too,' said Sam.

'Mine toooo,' said Harry from his cage which had been transferred to their cottage after a fracas in the centre when the cage was knocked over.

'I've been to three gay weddings,' said Mark. 'But that's Surrey for you.'

Then Angie recalled the fumbled kiss on board the Harvest Store. Perhaps it wasn't him retracting from a student-supervisor role after all. The saxophone, a masculine sort of brass instrument, the fishing, it didn't seem to add up. But these were only excuses. The truth was Angie had been blind to the reality, Kevin was gay.

◆

The following month Angie received a letter from Tony's solicitor. It referred to The Late Anthony Hendry Arnold. The legal firm, Henderson Primrose and Walker, had overseen his affairs since he left prison and had drawn up his Will. Retaining expenses for the funeral and the firm's fee of £514.90 for services rendered, Tony's Schedule of Estate amounted to £11,600. The cheque was drawn from the Glasgow Gorbals TSB branch and made out to Dr Angela Lawrence. In small print Angie noted that the sum of £350 was retained in Premium bonds and would remain open for another year before encashment.

Next day, Angie texted Mark informing him of his half of the estate and notified him that the cheque would be arriving soon, in Claygate. In his response, he asked if they could recommend either a hotel or B&B for his family to spend their summer holiday on Orkney.

♦

It was on a sunny May evening when two rhododendrons bushes were in glorious regal bloom Sam and Angie walked along the beach in a nonchalant manner. Arthur plodded along behind them as if trying to overhear their chatter. They walked hand in hand as the early summer sun dipped behind Saviskaill Head leaving a warm red glow for the morrow. They each kicked the seaweed aside as they progressed, then kicked off their shoes. Angie seemed deep in thought.

'The gulls, they take away the kids ailments. They let go of them in mid Atlantic and drown them.'

'A nice thought,' said Sam who could think of no other way progress could be made in her work.

They turned to see lights being put on in the centre and children running around. Their high unbroken voices shrieked and the wind carried their excitement to their ears on the shore.

'They can be boisterous that current crowd you've got now Angie,' said Sam.

'Yes. They are experiencing freedom. For some, the very first time."

'And we're experiencing something new for the very first time,' said Sam.

'And that is?' she asked.

'Gone are the daemons which controlled your life.'

'Yes that's true.'

'And you are now in a happier place with a real brother, a sister-in-law, a niece and a nephew. And before it was too late, you found your father.'

Angie's mouth felt dry.

'There's only one thing missing,' she said.

Sam recalled what he had just said.

'Nop, I think I covered all the ground.'

'The other one is you. Thanks for standing by me throughout my crazy journey.'

Sam spun Angie round.

'You are no longer the crazy psychologist,' and gave her a prolonged kiss.

Arthur did not like their statuary position and impatiently barked.

A skua made its way home to an offshore island out of sight and the waves gently progressed towards four feet silently sinking into wet sand. And still they kissed.

THE END

About the Author

Miller Caldwell is a Scottish based writer of novels, biographies, self-help and children's books. He graduated from London University having studied African spacial development, traditional African religions and the Colonial history of West Africa. He says it is when the attendant spirit of creativity descends that he writes the next book and that determines its genre. He has had articles published in Health magazines, The Scottish Review and his poetry and short stories regularly feature in The Fankle.

In a life of humanitarian work in Ghana, Pakistan and Scotland, he has gained remarkable insights into human nature through confronting Osama bin Laden near Abbotobad in 2006 and bringing an African dictator to tears in West Africa in 2000. He is the vice chair of the Scottish Association for the Study of Offending and a volunteer with the Cinnamon Trust caring for the pets of the terminally ill.

Miller plays a variety of brass, woodwind and keyboard instruments. They provide a break from writing but they sometimes feature in his books. His interest in UK and foreign ornithology fly into his work at times too. Married, he has two daughters and lives in Dumfries.

He currently serves on the committee of the Society of Authors in Scotland and is a member of the Children's Authors in the UK Society of Authors.

SPOT CHECK

- French or Italian Food   French 60% Italian 40%
- TV or Theatre   Theatre
- Late Night or Early Riser   Late Night
- Opera or Soap   Opera
- Cooking or being cooked   Cooking
  for
- Sand or snow   Both but not at the same time
- Beethoven or Beastie Boys   Beethoven
- Harrods or M&S   M&S I live in Dumfries
- Dog or Cat   Dog
- Telephone or e-mail   e-mail always please
- Whisky or Horlicks   Has to be Horlicks I rarely drink alcohol
- Five-star hotel or B&B?   B&B
- Tea or coffee   1 coffee in the morning then tea all day.
- Royals or Politicians   Politicians are more interesting
- Jamie Oliver or Mrs Beeton   Both
- Starter or pudding   Heart says pudding; mind says starter
- I couldn't get through the weekend without....   Match of the Day.

Interview

Why write about a profession you profess to know very little about?

That was indeed a challenge. But do you have to be a criminal to write a crime story? I know several Clinical Psychologists and felt comfortable dipping into their profession as I wrote. Of course I have created a bizarre if not completely unprofessional personality in Angie. This is not a text book, of course, but The Crazy Psychologist. I don't think in real life many psychologists can claim to be that.

Do you always know how your stories will end?

No. I know the boundaries of the story. I create the characters and places but the story line is the path of a snake. The secret is to go from start to finish on a central premise but go down byways to explore and colour the story with doubts and possibilities but never lose the theme.

With an awkward protagonist, how did you make her loveable?

Even the most admired individual has some faults. We all

do. Angie's faults come from a disadvantaged and cruel childhood where we sympathise with her and by doing so, we bond with her and begin to understand what drives her in her work and pleasure. We follow her journey which does end in happiness on several different levels. Not least to her long suffering husband.

Most of your books feature animals or birds in them. Why is that?

In my children's books, animals are very popular. In my biographies it is because they existed. In my novels they are part of the colour and personality which adds to our pleasure in our often stressed and anxious world. The extent of animals mentioned varies in each book and is only used when they enhance the story. A Basset Hound and an African Grey Parrot seem to have characteristics which fit well in an assessment centre for troubled children.

Your last novel, The Parrot's Tale, was 400 pages. Why is this one half that size?

The length of a story should be what it requires. A short story would not be improved if it was a 400 page block buster. Ian Rankine once said that a book should be as long as it needs to be. This novel, or if you prefer novella, is such an example.

What will be your next book ?

My next book will be an academic book about Industrial Mission in Africa. My next children's book, Danny the Spotless Dalmatian, will be published next year.

Dumfries Dec 2014

Miller's Other Books

Novels
>Operation Oboe
>The Last Shepherd
>Restless Waves
>Miss Martha Douglas
>The Parrot's Tale
>The Crazy Psychologist

Biographies
>Untied Laces
>Jim's Retiring Collection
>Poet's Progeny
>7 point 7 on the Richter Scale
>Take The Lead

Children's Books
>Chaz the Friendly Crocodile
>Lawrence the Lion Seeks Work
>Danny the Spotless Dalmatian

Self Help
>Have you seen my Ummm...Memory?
>Ponderings - IN LARGE PRINT
>It's Me Honest It Is - NHS booklet